Phyllis Michael

The Works of
"Saki"
(H. H. Munro)

The Westminster Alice
Reginald and *Reginald in Russia*
The Chronicles of Clovis
The Unbearable Bassington
When William Came
Beasts and Super-Beasts
The Toys of Peace
The Square Egg

THE WORKS OF

"SAKI"

(H. H. MUNRO)

BIBLIOGRAPHICAL NOTE

First Published 1914
Reprinted 1922
Collected Edition 1926
Reprinted 1927
Reprinted 1928
Reprinted 1928
Reprinted 1929
Reprinted 1930

BEASTS & SUPER-BEASTS

by

"SAKI" (H. H. MUNRO)

with an Introduction by

H. W. NEVINSON

JOHN LANE
THE BODLEY HEAD LTD

Made and Printed in Great Britain by Butler & Tanner Ltd., Frome and London

INTRODUCTION

THE first time I met "Saki" was in St. Petersburg during the attempted revolution of 1905. We were staying in the same hotel, I as correspondent of the *Daily Chronicle*, he, I think, of the *Morning Post*. At all events he ought to have been for the *Morning Post*, since he was endowed with just the right touch of "educated scorn" which has always distinguished that superior paper. Like his paper, "Saki" was suspicious of all enthusiasm, especially of all Liberal enthusiasm, and stood ready to mock at the zeal and aspirations of all "faddists" and "cranks." His nature ranged him on the side of authority and tradition, while he despised the ideals of "progress" as amiable illusions. One saw the twist of cynicism clearly marked on his face. His aspect of the world was cynical. But the cynicism was humorous and charming, partly assumed as a protective covering to conceal and shelter feeling. That is our English way, and in the suppression of emotion, or of its outward signs, "Saki" was entirely English.

Even in these stories, so far removed from politics, one comes suddenly upon this shrewd distrust of theories and reforming ideals. Consider that sharp stroke in "The Treasure Ship":

"Somewhere on the west coast of Ireland the Dulverton property included a few acres of shingle, rock, and heather, too barren to support even an agrarian outrage."

Or consider the precautions of the lady who wished to give the candidate for election (obviously a Liberal) a respite from politics in "The Lull":

"I've had the picture of Cromwell dissolving the Long Parliament taken down from the staircase, and even the portrait of Lord Rosebery's 'Ladas' removed from the smoking-room."

Or take that phrase in "The Unkindest Blow":

"The Government of the day, which from its tendency to be a few hours behind the course of events had been nicknamed the Government of the afternoon, was obliged to intervene with promptitude and decision."

Or the description of the lady who was a Socialist by conviction:

"When she inveighed eloquently against the evils of capitalism at drawing-room meetings and Fabian Conferences she was conscious of a comfortable feeling that the system, with all its inequalities and iniquities, would probably last her time. It is one of the consolations of middle-aged reformers that the good they inculcate must live after them if it is to live at all."

There you get the pure satiric irony, and you will

find more than a touch of it whenever Trade Unions and Strikes come into the story, as in that same " Byzantine Omelette " or " The Unkindest Blow." Something similar is the educated scorn of the vulgar herd in " Cousin Teresa," with its wildly popular refrain of " The Big Borzoi."

In fact, the charm of cynical sanity enters into nearly all " Saki's " inventions. Rather than admit saints and heroes to sentimental adoration he tinges nearly all his characters with a delightful malice. In " The Story-Teller " he lets us into his own secret. There we are shown to perfection the nature of children and their persistent, unanswerable questions (" Why is the grass in the other field better ? " and so on). But we also see the dislike that children and all human beings instinctively feel towards the uncommonly good, and the general joy when an evil fate overtakes them owing to their goodness. For if Bertha's three medals for goodness had not clinked together, the wolf would not have found and devoured her, and what a pity that would have been !

A delightful and ingenious wickedness gives a charm to nearly all the stories, and it is noticeable that the most wickedly malicious of the characters are dear, innocent little girls or even good, sweet women who ought to have been " ministering angel thous." On the whole, I think I like the girl in " The Lull " best. Her idea of distracting the politician's mind by bringing a little pig and a gamecock into his bedroom is most ingenious. And then her description of the imaginary flood that made the shelter necessary :

" Good gracious ! Have any lives been lost ? "

" Heaps, I should say. The second housemaid has already identified three bodies that have floated past the billiard-room window as being the young man she's engaged to. Either she's engaged to a large assortment of the population round here or else she's very careless at identification. Of course it may be the same body coming round again and again in a swirl ; I hadn't thought of that."

And I love Matilda in " The Boar-Pig " story. Minx, liar, thief—— Oh, yes ! I know all that. But how ingenious ! How lovable !

" Shoo ! Hish ! Hish ! Shoo ! " cried the ladies in chorus.

" If they think they're going to drive him away by reciting lists of the kings of Israel and Judah they're laying themselves out for disappointment," observed Matilda from her seat in the medlar tree.

Equally fine is the mendacious invention of Vera in " The Quince Tree." The malice of Eleanor in " Fur " almost surpasses her charm, but how pleasing is the final remark :

" A cloud has arisen between the friendships of the two young women ; as far as Eleanor is concerned the cloud has a silver-fox lining."

One naturally classes Max Beerbohm with " Saki." Their half-humorous, half-cynical attitude of mind is much the same. But even Max is not so consummate a liar as "Saki." I suppose "Saki" is the finest liar in literature. In "The Way of All Flesh" Samuel Butler showed himself a good liar, but his lies are not so rich in invention as "Saki's." Which is the most outrageous lie in this lot? It is hard to decide between "The Lull," already mentioned, "The Hen," "The Romancers," and "A Defensive Diamond." But on the whole I incline to "The Schartz-Metterklume Method." That has all the advantages of a splendid lie and a series of surprises. Surprise is one of "Saki's" favourite jests. In that story how startling is the answer of the pseudo-governess:

"We got very satisfactory references about you from Canon Teep," she (Mrs. Quabarl, the employer) observed: "a very estimable man, I should think."

"Drinks like a fish and beats his wife, otherwise a very lovable character," said the governess imperturbably.

And then I like the lie and the surprise in "Dusk." The story is so nearly a commonplace tract, but how charmingly it is saved by the malicious surprise of the last six words.

For mere wit of expression one might take the description of the Duke of Falvertoon in "The Unkindest Blow" (not in itself the best of the stories), as "One of those human *hors d'œuvres* that stimulate the public appetite for sensation without giving it much to feed on." Or of the soft and idle young man who was "one of those people who would be enormously improved by death" ("The Feats of Nemesis"). And what perfection of satire on the artistic taste of the British public is hidden in the account of Eshley (in "The Stalled Ox") who won success by painting cattle drowsing picturesquely under walnut-trees, and was obliged by the public to go on painting the same subject for ever. How well I remember a Royal Academician who painted a cow by a willowy stream about the middle of last century and for fifty or sixty years continued to paint that cow beside a willowy stream without noticeable variation or sign of age.

There is only one tragic story in this collection ("The Cobweb"), and a reader should be warned against swallowing the whole succession rapidly one after the other. That dulls the appetite for the wit and malice. It is worse than reading a whole volume of an old *Punch* on end, and there is little more depressing than that. "Saki" must be taken as an occasional spice, an exquisite *aperitif*. He is best as a defence against commonplace and sentimentality. To myself his works, like his conversation, have given so many happy moments that when I think with sorrow upon the friends that I lost in the war, his small and twisted face, in expression like a young and humorous bird's, stands among the first that rise before my mind. It stands beside Rupert Brooke's and Edward Thomas's.

HENRY W. NEVINSON.

AUTHOR'S NOTE

"THE Open Window," "The Schartz-Metterklume Method," and "Clovis on Parental Responsibilities," originally appeared in the *Westminster Gazette*, "The Elk" in the *Bystander*, and the remaining stories in the *Morning Post*. To the Editors of these papers I am indebted for their courtesy in allowing me to reprint them.

H. H. M.

CONTENTS

CONTENTS

BEASTS AND SUPER-BEASTS

BEASTS AND SUPER-BEASTS

THE SHE-WOLF

LEONARD BILSITER was one of those people who have failed to find this world attractive or interesting, and who have sought compensation in an "unseen world" of their own experience or imagination—or invention. Children do that sort of thing successfully, but children are content to convince themselves, and do not vulgarize their beliefs by trying to convince other people. Leonard Bilsiter's beliefs were for "the few," that is to say, anyone who would listen to him.

His dabblings in the unseen might not have carried him beyond the customary platitudes of the drawing-room visionary if accident had not reinforced his stock-in-trade of mystical lore. In company with a friend, who was interested in a Ural mining concern, he had made a trip across Eastern Europe at a moment when the great Russian railway strike was developing from a threat to a reality; its outbreak caught him on the return journey, somewhere on the further side of Perm, and it was while waiting for a couple of days at a wayside station in a state of suspended locomotion that he made the acquaintance of a dealer in harness and metalware, who profitably whiled away the tedium of the long halt by initiating his

English travelling companion in a fragmentary system of folk-lore that he had picked up from Trans-Baikal traders and natives. Leonard returned to his home circle garrulous about his Russian strike experiences, but oppressively reticent about certain dark mysteries, which he alluded to under the resounding title of Siberian Magic. The reticence wore off in a week or two under the influence of an entire lack of general curiosity, and Leonard began to make more detailed allusions to the enormous powers which this new esoteric force, to use his own description of it, conferred on the initiated few who knew how to wield it. His aunt, Cecilia Hoops, who loved sensation perhaps rather better than she loved the truth, gave him as clamorous an advertisement as anyone could wish for by retailing an account of how he had turned a vegetable marrow into a wood-pigeon before her very eyes. As a manifestation of the possession of supernatural powers, the story was discounted in some quarters by the respect accorded to Mrs. Hoops' powers of imagination.

However divided opinion might be on the question of Leonard's status as a wonderworker or a charlatan, he certainly arrived at Mary Hampton's house-party with a reputation for pre-eminence in one or other of those professions, and he was not disposed to shun such publicity as might fall to his share. Esoteric forces and unusual powers figured largely in whatever conversation he or his aunt had a share in, and his own performances, past and potential, were the subject of mysterious hints and dark avowals.

"I wish you would turn me into a wolf, Mr. Bilsiter," said his hostess at luncheon the day after his arrival.

"My dear Mary," said Colonel Hampton, "I never knew you had a craving in that direction."

"A she-wolf, of course," continued Mrs. Hampton; "it would be too confusing to change one's sex as well as one's species at a moment's notice."

"I don't think one should jest on these subjects," said Leonard.

"I'm not jesting, I'm quite serious, I assure you. Only don't do it to-day; we have only eight available bridge players, and it would break up one of our tables. To-morrow we shall be a larger party. To-morrow night, after dinner——"

"In our present imperfect understanding of these hidden forces I think one should approach them with humbleness rather than mockery," observed Leonard, with such severity that the subject was forthwith dropped.

Clovis Sangrail had sat unusually silent during the discussion on the possibilities of Siberian Magic; after lunch he side-tracked Lord Pabham into the comparative seclusion of the billiard-room and delivered himself of a searching question.

"Have you such a thing as a she-wolf in your collection of wild animals? A she-wolf of moderately good temper?"

Lord Pabham considered. "There is Louisa," he said, "a rather fine specimen of the timber-wolf. I got her two years ago in exchange for some Arctic foxes. Most of my animals get to be fairly tame before they've been with me very long; I think I can say Louisa has an angelic temper, as she-wolves go. Why do you ask?"

"I was wondering whether you would lend her to me for to-morrow night," said Clovis, with the careless solicitude of one who borrows a collar stud or a tennis racquet.

"To-morrow night?"

"Yes, wolves are nocturnal animals, so the late hours won't hurt her," said Clovis, with the air of one who has taken everything into consideration; "one of your men could bring her over from Pabham Park after dusk, and with a little help he ought to be able to smuggle her into the conservatory at the same moment that Mary Hampton makes an unobtrusive exit."

Lord Pabham stared at Clovis for a moment in pardonable bewilderment; then his face broke into a wrinkled network of laughter.

"Oh, that's your game, is it? You are going to do a little Siberian Magic on your own account. And is Mrs. Hampton willing to be a fellow-conspirator?"

"Mary is pledged to see me through with it, if you will guarantee Louisa's temper."

"I'll answer for Louisa," said Lord Pabham.

By the following day the house-party had swollen to larger proportions, and Bilsiter's instinct for self-advertisement expanded duly under the stimulant of an increased audience. At dinner that evening he held forth at length on the subject of unseen forces and untested powers, and his flow of impressive eloquence continued unabated while coffee was being served in the drawing-room preparatory to a general migration to the card-room. His aunt ensured a respectful hearing for his utterances, but her sensation-loving soul hankered after something more dramatic than mere vocal demonstration.

"Won't you do something to *convince* them of your powers, Leonard?" she pleaded; "change something into another shape. He can, you know, if he only chooses to," she informed the company.

"Oh, do," said Mavis Pellington earnestly, and her request was echoed by nearly every one present. Even those who were not open to conviction were perfectly willing to be entertained by an exhibition of amateur conjuring.

Leonard felt that something tangible was expected of him.

"Has anyone present," he asked, "got a threepenny bit or some small object of no particular value——?"

"You're surely not going to make coins disappear, or something primitive of that sort?" said Clovis contemptuously.

"I think it very unkind of you not to carry out my suggestion of turning me into a wolf," said Mary Hampton, as she crossed over to the conservatory to give her macaws their usual tribute from the dessert dishes.

"I have already warned you of the danger of treating these powers in a mocking spirit," said Leonard solemnly.

"I don't believe you can do it," laughed Mary provocatively from the conservatory; "I dare you to do it if you can. I defy you to turn me into a wolf."

As she said this she was lost to view behind a clump of azaleas.

"Mrs. Hampton——" began Leonard with increased solemnity, but he got no further. A breath of chill air seemed to rush across the room, and at the same time the macaws broke forth into ear-splitting screams.

"What on earth is the matter with those confounded

birds, Mary ?" exclaimed Colonel Hampton ; at the same moment an even more piercing scream from Mavis Pellington stampeded the entire company from their seats. In various attitudes of helpless horror or instinctive defence they confronted the evil-looking grey beast that was peering at them from amid a setting of fern and azalea.

Mrs. Hoops was the first to recover from the general chaos of fright and bewilderment.

"Leonard !" she screamed shrilly to her nephew, "turn it back into Mrs. Hampton at once ! It may fly at us at any moment. Turn it back !"

"I—I don't know how to," faltered Leonard, who looked more scared and horrified than anyone.

"What !" shouted Colonel Hampton, "you've taken the abominable liberty of turning my wife into a wolf, and now you stand there calmly and say you can't turn her back again !"

To do strict justice to Leonard, calmness was not a distinguishing feature of his attitude at the moment.

"I assure you I didn't turn Mrs. Hampton into a wolf ; nothing was farther from my intentions," he protested.

"Then where is she, and how came that animal into the conservatory ?" demanded the Colonel.

"Of course we must accept your assurance that you didn't turn Mrs. Hampton into a wolf," said Clovis politely, "but you will agree that appearances are against you."

"Are we to have all these recriminations with that beast standing there ready to tear us to pieces ?" wailed Mavis indignantly.

"Lord Pabham, you know a good deal about wild beasts——" suggested Colonel Hampton.

"The wild beasts that I have been accustomed to," said Lord Pabham, "have come with proper credentials from well-known dealers, or have been bred in my own menagerie. I've never before been confronted with an animal that walks unconcernedly out of an azalea bush, leaving a charming and popular hostess unaccounted for. As far as one can judge from *outward* characteristics," he continued, "it has the appearance of a well-grown female of the North American timber-wolf, a variety of the common species *canis lupus*."

"Oh, never mind its Latin name," screamed Mavis, as the beast came a step or two further into the room; "can't you entice it away with food, and shut it up where it can't do any harm?"

"If it is really Mrs. Hampton, who has just had a very good dinner, I don't suppose food will appeal to it very strongly," said Clovis.

"Leonard," beseeched Mrs. Hoops tearfully, "even if this *is* none of your doing can't you use your great powers to turn this dreadful beast into something harmless before it bites us all—a rabbit or something?"

"I don't suppose Colonel Hampton would care to have his wife turned into a succession of fancy animals as though we were playing a round game with her," interposed Clovis.

"I absolutely forbid it," thundered the Colonel.

"Most wolves that I've had anything to do with have been inordinately fond of sugar," said Lord Pabham; "if you like I'll try the effect on this one."

He took a piece of sugar from the saucer of his coffee cup and flung it to the expectant Louisa, who snapped it in mid-air. There was a sigh of relief from the company; a wolf that ate sugar when it might at the least have been employed in tearing macaws to pieces had already shed some of its terrors. The sigh deepened to a gasp of thanksgiving when Lord Pabham decoyed the animal out of the room by a pretended largesse of further sugar. There was an instant rush to the vacated conservatory. There was no trace of Mrs. Hampton except the plate containing the macaws' supper.

"The door is locked on the inside!" exclaimed Clovis, who had deftly turned the key as he affected to test it.

Every one turned towards Bilsiter.

"If you haven't turned my wife into a wolf," said Colonel Hampton, "will you kindly explain where she has disappeared to, since she obviously could not have gone through a locked door? I will not press you for an explanation of how a North American timber-wolf suddenly appeared in the conservatory, but I think I have some right to inquire what has become of Mrs. Hampton."

Bilsiter's reiterated disclaimer was met with a general murmur of impatient disbelief.

"I refuse to stay another hour under this roof," declared Mavis Pellington.

"If our hostess has really vanished out of human form," said Mrs. Hoops, "none of the ladies of the party can very well remain. I absolutely decline to be chaperoned by a wolf!"

"It's a she-wolf," said Clovis soothingly.

The correct etiquette to be observed under the unusual circumstances received no further elucidation. The sudden entry of Mary Hampton deprived the discussion of its immediate interest.

"Some one has mesmerized me," she exclaimed

crossly; "I found myself in the game larder, of all places, being fed with sugar by Lord Pabham. I hate being mesmerized, and the doctor has forbidden me to touch sugar."

The situation was explained to her, as far as it permitted of anything that could be called explanation.

"Then you *really* did turn me into a wolf, Mr. Bilsiter?" she exclaimed excitedly.

But Leonard had burned the boat in which he might now have embarked on a sea of glory. He could only shake his head feebly.

"It was I who took that liberty," said Clovis; "you see, I happen to have lived for a couple of years in North-Eastern Russia, and I have more than a tourist's acquaintance with the magic craft of that region. One does not care to speak about these strange powers, but once in a way, when one hears a lot of nonsense being talked about them, one is tempted to show what Siberian magic can accomplish in the hands of some one who really understands it. I yielded to that temptation. May I have some brandy? the effort has left me rather faint."

If Leonard Bilsiter could at that moment have transformed Clovis into a cockroach and then have stepped on him he would gladly have performed both operations.

LAURA

"YOU are not really dying, are you?" asked Amanda.

"I have the doctor's permission to live till Tuesday," said Laura.

"But to-day is Saturday; this is serious!" gasped Amanda.

"I don't know about it being serious; it is certainly Saturday," said Laura.

"Death is always serious," said Amanda.

"I never said I was going to die. I am presumably going to leave off being Laura, but I shall go on being something. An animal of some kind, I suppose. You see, when one hasn't been very good in the life one has just lived, one reincarnates in some lower organism. And I haven't been very good, when one comes to think of it. I've been petty and mean and vindictive and all that sort of thing when circumstances have seemed to warrant it."

"Circumstances never warrant that sort of thing," said Amanda hastily.

"If you don't mind my saying so," observed Laura, "Egbert is a circumstance that would warrant any amount of that sort of thing. You're married to him—that's different; you've sworn to love, honour, and endure him: I haven't."

"I don't see what's wrong with Egbert," protested Amanda

"Oh, I dare say the wrongness has been on my part," admitted Laura dispassionately; "he has merely been the extenuating circumstance. He made a thin, peevish kind of fuss, for instance, when I took the collie puppies from the farm out for a run the other day."

"They chased his young broods of speckled Sussex and drove two sitting hens off their nests, besides running all over the flower beds. You know how devoted he is to his poultry and garden."

"Anyhow, he needn't have gone on about it for the entire evening and then have said, 'Let's say no more about it' just when I was beginning to enjoy the discussion. That's where one of my petty vindictive revenges came in," added Laura with an unrepentant chuckle; "I turned the entire family of speckled Sussex into his seedling shed the day after the puppy episode."

"How could you?" exclaimed Amanda.

"It came quite easy," said Laura; "two of the hens pretended to be laying at the time, but I was firm."

"And we thought it was an accident!"

"You see," resumed Laura, "I really *have* some grounds for supposing that my next incarnation will be in a lower organism. I shall be an animal of some kind. On the other hand, I haven't been a bad sort in my way, so I think I may count on being a nice animal, something elegant and lively, with a love of fun. An otter, perhaps."

"I can't imagine you as an otter," said Amanda.

"Well, I don't suppose you can imagine me as an angel, if it comes to that," said Laura.

Amanda was silent. She couldn't.

"Personally I think an otter life would be rather enjoyable," continued Laura; "salmon to eat all the year round, and the satisfaction of being able to fetch the trout in their own homes without having to wait for hours till they condescend to rise to the fly you've been dangling before them; and an elegant svelte figure——"

"Think of the otter hounds," interposed Amanda; "how dreadful to be hunted and harried and finally worried to death!"

"Rather fun with half the neighbourhood looking on, and anyhow not worse than this Saturday-to-Tuesday business of dying by inches; and then I should go on into something else. If I had been a moderately good otter I suppose I should get back into human shape of some sort; probably something rather primitive—a little brown, unclothed Nubian boy, I should think."

"I wish you would be serious," sighed Amanda; "you really ought to be if you're only going to live till Tuesday."

As a matter of fact Laura died on Monday.

"So dreadfully upsetting," Amanda complained to her uncle-in-law, Sir Lulworth Quayne. "I've asked quite a lot of people down for golf and fishing, and the rhododendrons are just looking their best."

"Laura always was inconsiderate," said Sir Lulworth; "she was born during Goodwood week, with an Ambassador staying in the house who hated babies."

"She had the maddest kind of ideas," said Amanda; "do you know if there was any insanity in her family?"

"Insanity? No, I never heard of any. Her father lives in West Kensington, but I believe he's sane on all other subjects."

"She had an idea that she was going to be reincarnated as an otter," said Amanda.

"One meets with those ideas of reincarnation so frequently, even in the West," said Sir Lulworth, "that one can hardly set them down as being mad. And Laura was such an unaccountable person in this life that I should not like to lay down definite rules as to what she might be doing in an after state."

"You think she really might have passed into some animal form?" asked Amanda. She was one of those who shape their opinions rather readily from the standpoint of those around them.

Just then Egbert entered the breakfast-room, wearing an air of bereavement that Laura's demise would have been insufficient, in itself, to account for.

"Four of my speckled Sussex have been killed," he exclaimed; "the very four that were to go to the show on Friday. One of them was dragged away and eaten right in the middle of that new carnation bed that I've been to such trouble and expense over. My best flower bed and my best fowls singled out for destruction; it almost seems as if the brute that did the deed had special knowledge how to be as devastating as possible in a short space of time."

"Was it a fox, do you think?" asked Amanda.

"Sounds more like a polecat," said Sir Lulworth.

"No," said Egbert, "there were marks of webbed feet all over the place, and we followed the tracks down to the stream at the bottom of the garden; evidently an otter."

Amanda looked quickly and furtively across at Sir Lulworth.

Egbert was too agitated to eat any breakfast, and

went out to superintend the strengthening of the poultry yard defences.

"I think she might at least have waited till the funeral was over," said Amanda in a scandalized voice.

"It's her own funeral, you know," said Sir Lulworth; "it's a nice point in etiquette how far one ought to show respect to one's own mortal remains."

Disregard for mortuary convention was carried to further lengths next day; during the absence of the family at the funeral ceremony the remaining survivors of the speckled Sussex were massacred. The marauder's line of retreat seemed to have embraced most of the flower beds on the lawn, but the strawberry beds in the lower garden had also suffered.

"I shall get the otter hounds to come here at the earliest possible moment," said Egbert savagely.

"On no account! You can't dream of such a thing!" exclaimed Amanda. "I mean, it wouldn't do, so soon after a funeral in the house."

"It's a case of necessity," said Egbert; "once an otter takes to that sort of thing it won't stop."

"Perhaps it will go elsewhere now that there are no more fowls left," suggested Amanda.

"One would think you wanted to shield the beast," said Egbert.

"There's been so little water in the stream lately," objected Amanda; "it seems hardly sporting to hunt an animal when it has so little chance of taking refuge anywhere."

"Good gracious!" fumed Egbert, "I'm not thinking about sport. I want to have the animal killed as soon as possible."

Even Amanda's opposition weakened when, during

church time on the following Sunday, the otter made its way into the house, raided half a salmon from the larder and worried it into scaly fragments on the Persian rug in Egbert's studio.

"We shall have it hiding under our beds and biting pieces out of our feet before long," said Egbert, and from what Amanda knew of this particular otter she felt that the possibility was not a remote one.

On the evening preceding the day fixed for the hunt Amanda spent a solitary hour walking by the banks of the stream, making what she imagined to be hound noises. It was charitably supposed by those who overheard her performance, that she was practising for farmyard imitations at the forthcoming village entertainment.

It was her friend and neighbour, Aurora Burret, who brought her news of the day's sport.

"Pity you weren't out; we had quite a good day. We found at once, in the pool just below your garden."

"Did you—kill?" asked Amanda.

"Rather. A fine she-otter. Your husband got rather badly bitten in trying to 'tail it.' Poor beast, I felt quite sorry for it, it had such a human look in its eyes when it was killed. You'll call me silly, but do you know who the look reminded me of? My dear woman, what is the matter?"

When Amanda had recovered to a certain extent from her attack of nervous prostration Egbert took her to the Nile Valley to recuperate. Change of scene speedily brought about the desired recovery of health and mental balance. The escapades of an adventurous otter in search of a variation of diet were viewed in their proper light. Amanda's normally placid temperament reasserted itself. Even a hurricane of shouted curses, coming from her husband's dressing-room, in her husband's voice, but hardly in his usual vocabulary, failed to disturb her serenity as she made a leisurely toilet one evening in a Cairo hotel.

"What is the matter? What has happened?" she asked in amused curiosity.

"The little beast has thrown all my clean shirts into the bath! Wait till I catch you, you little——"

"What little beast?" asked Amanda, suppressing a desire to laugh; Egbert's language was so hopelessly inadequate to express his outraged feelings.

"A little beast of a naked brown Nubian boy," spluttered Egbert.

And now Amanda is seriously ill.

THE BOAR-PIG

"THERE is a back way on to the lawn," said Mrs. Philidore Stossen to her daughter, "through a small grass paddock and then through a walled fruit garden full of gooseberry bushes. I went all over the place last year when the family were away. There is a door that opens from the fruit garden into a shrubbery, and once we emerge from there we can mingle with the guests as if we had come in by the ordinary way. It's much safer than going in by the front entrance and running the risk of coming bang up against the hostess; that would be so awkward when she doesn't happen to have invited us."

"Isn't it a lot of trouble to take for getting admittance to a garden party?"

"To a garden party, yes; to *the* garden party of the season, certainly not. Every one of any consequence in the county, with the exception of ourselves, has been asked to meet the Princess, and it would be far more troublesome to invent explanations as to why we weren't there than to get in by a roundabout way. I stopped Mrs. Cuvering in the road yesterday and talked very pointedly about the Princess. If she didn't choose to take the hint and send me an invitation it's not my fault, is it? Here we are: we just cut across the grass and through that little gate into the garden."

Mrs. Stossen and her daughter, suitably arrayed for

a county garden party function with an infusion of Almanack de Gotha, sailed through the narrow grass paddock and the ensuing gooseberry garden with the air of state barges making an unofficial progress along a rural trout stream. There was a certain amount of furtive haste mingled with the stateliness of their advance as though hostile searchlights might be turned on them at any moment; and, as a matter of fact, they were not unobserved. Matilda Cuvering, with the alert eyes of thirteen years old and the added advantage of an exalted position in the branches of a medlar tree, had enjoyed a good view of the Stossen flanking movement and had foreseen exactly where it would break down in execution.

"They'll find the door locked, and they'll jolly well have to go back the way they came," she remarked to herself. "Serves them right for not coming in by the proper entrance. What a pity Tarquin Superbus isn't loose in the paddock. After all, as every one else is enjoying themselves, I don't see why Tarquin shouldn't have an afternoon out."

Matilda was of an age when thought is action; she slid down from the branches of the medlar tree, and when she clambered back again, Tarquin, the huge white Yorkshire boar-pig, had exchanged the narrow limits of his sty for the wider range of the grass paddock. The discomfited Stossen expedition, returning in recriminatory but otherwise orderly retreat from the unyielding obstacle of the locked door, came to a sudden halt at the gate dividing the paddock from the gooseberry garden.

"What a villainous-looking animal," exclaimed Mrs. Stossen; "it wasn't there when we came in."

"It's there now, anyhow," said her daughter

"What on earth are we to do? I wish we had never come."

The boar-pig had drawn nearer to the gate for a closer inspection of the human intruders, and stood champing his jaws and blinking his small red eyes in a manner that was doubtless intended to be disconcerting, and, as far as the Stossens were concerned, thoroughly achieved that result.

"Shoo! Hish! Hish! Shoo!" cried the ladies in chorus.

"If they think they're going to drive him away by reciting lists of the kings of Israel and Judah they're laying themselves out for disappointment," observed Matilda from her seat in the medlar tree. As she made the observation aloud Mrs. Stossen became for the first time aware of her presence. A moment or two earlier she would have been anything but pleased at the discovery that the garden was not as deserted as it looked, but now she hailed the fact of the child's presence on the scene with absolute relief.

"Little girl, can you find some one to drive away ——" she began hopefully.

"*Comment? Comprends pas,*" was the response.

"Oh, are you French? *Êtes vous française?*"

"*Pas de tous. 'Suis anglaise.*"

"Then why not talk English? I want to know if——"

"*Permettez-moi expliquer.* You see, I'm rather under a cloud," said Matilda. "I'm staying with my aunt, and I was told I must behave particularly well to-day, as lots of people were coming for a garden party, and I was told to imitate Claude, that's my young cousin, who never does anything wrong except by accident, and then is always apologetic about it.

It seems they thought I ate too much raspberry trifle at lunch, and they said Claude never eats too much raspberry trifle. Well, Claude always goes to sleep for half an hour after lunch, because he's told to, and I waited till he was asleep, and tied his hands and started forcible feeding with a whole bucketful of raspberry trifle that they were keeping for the garden-party. Lots of it went on to his sailor-suit and some of it on to the bed, but a good deal went down Claude's throat, and they can't say again that he has never been known to eat too much raspberry trifle. That is why I am not allowed to go to the party, and as an additional punishment I must speak French all the afternoon. I've had to tell you all this in English, as there were words like 'forcible feeding' that I didn't know the French for; of course I could have invented them, but if I had said *nourriture obligatoire* you wouldn't have had the least idea what I was talking about. *Mais maintenant, nous parlons français.*"

"Oh, very well, *très bien*," said Mrs. Stossen reluctantly; in moments of flurry such French as she knew was not under very good control. "*Là, à l'autre côté de la porte, est un cochon*——"

"*Un cochon? Ah, le petit charmant!*" exclaimed Matilda with enthusiasm.

"*Mais non, pas du tout petit, et pas du tout charmant; un bête féroce*——"

"*Une bête*," corrected Matilda; "a pig is masculine as long as you call it a pig, but if you lose your temper with it and call it a ferocious beast it becomes one of us at once French is a dreadfully unsexing language."

"For goodness' sake let us talk English then," said Mrs. Stossen. "Is there any way out of this garden except through the paddock where the pig is?"

"I always go over the wall, by way of the plum tree," said Matilda.

"Dressed as we are we could hardly do that," said Mrs. Stossen; it was difficult to imagine her doing it in any costume.

"Do you think you could go and get some one who would drive the pig away?" saked Miss Stossen.

"I promised my aunt I would stay here till five o'clock; it's not four yet."

"I am sure, under the circumstances, your aunt would permit——"

"My conscience would not permit," said Matilda with cold dignity.

"We can't stay here till five o'clock," exclaimed Mrs. Stossen with growing exasperation.

"Shall I recite to you to make the time pass quicker?" asked Matilda obligingly. "'Belinda, the little Breadwinner,' is considered my best piece, or, perhaps, it ought to be something in French. Henri Quatre's address to his soldiers is the only thing I really know in that language."

"If you will go and fetch some one to drive that animal away I will give you something to buy yourself a nice present," said Mrs. Stossen.

Matilda came several inches lower down the medlar tree.

"That is the most practical suggestion you have made yet for getting out of the garden," she remarked cheerfully; "Claude and I are collecting money for the Children's Fresh Air Fund, and we are seeing which of us can collect the biggest sum."

"I shall be very glad to contribute half a crown, very glad indeed," said Mrs. Stossen, digging that coin out of the depths of a receptacle which formed a detached outwork of her toilet.

"Claude is a long way ahead of me at present," continued Matilda, taking no notice of the suggested offering; "you see, he's only eleven, and has golden hair, and those are enormous advantages when you're on the collecting job. Only the other day a Russian lady gave him ten shillings. Russians understand the art of giving far better than we do. I expect Claude will net quite twenty-five shillings this afternoon; he'll have the field to himself, and he'll be able to do the pale, fragile, not-long-for-this-world business to perfection after his raspberry trifle experience. Yes, he'll be *quite* two pounds ahead of me by now."

With much probing and plucking and many regretful murmurs the beleaguered ladies managed to produce seven-and-sixpence between them.

"I am afraid this is all we've got," said Mrs. Stossen.

Matilda showed no sign of coming down either to the earth or to their figure.

"I could not do violence to my conscience for anything less than ten shillings," she announced stiffly.

Mother and daughter muttered certain remarks under their breath, in which the word "beast" was prominent, and probably had no reference to Tarquin.

"I find I *have* got another half-crown," said Mrs. Stossen in a shaking voice; "here you are. Now please fetch some one quickly."

Matilda slipped down from the tree, took possession of the donation, and proceeded to pick up a handful of over-ripe medlars from the grass at her feet. Then she climbed over the gate and addressed herself affectionately to the boar-pig.

"Come, Tarquin, dear old boy; you know you

can't resist medlars when they're rotten and squashy."

Tarquin couldn't. By dint of throwing the fruit in front of him at judicious intervals Matilda decoyed him back to his sty, while the delivered captives hurried across the paddock.

"Well, I never! The little minx!" exclaimed Mrs. Stossen when she was safely on the high road. "The animal wasn't savage at all, and as for the ten shillings, I don't believe the Fresh Air Fund will see a penny of it!"

There she was unwarrantably harsh in her judgment. If you examine the books of the fund you will find the acknowledgment: "Collected by Miss Matilda Cuvering, 2s. 6d."

THE BROGUE

THE hunting season had come to an end, and the Mullets had not succeeded in selling the Brogue. There had been a kind of tradition in the family for the past three or four years, a sort of fatalistic hope, that the Brogue would find a purchaser before the hunting was over; but seasons came and went without anything happening to justify such ill-founded optimism. The animal had been named Berserker in the earlier stages of its career; it had been re-christened the Brogue later on, in recognition of the fact that, once acquired, it was extremely difficult to get rid of. The unkinder wits of the neighbourhood had been known to suggest that the first letter of its name was superfluous. The Brogue had been variously described in sale catalogues as a light-weight hunter, a lady's hack, and, more simply, but still with a touch of imagination, as a useful brown gelding, standing 15.1. Toby Mullet had ridden him for four seasons with the West Wessex; you can ride almost any sort of horse with the West Wessex as long as it is an animal that knows the country. The Brogue knew the country intimately, having personally created most of the gaps that were to be met with in banks and hedges for many miles round. His manners and characteristics were not ideal in the hunting field, but he was probably rather safer to ride to hounds than he was as a hack on country roads. According to the Mullet family, he was not really road-shy, but there were one or two objects of dislike that brought on sudden attacks of what Toby called swerving sickness. Motors and cycles he treated with tolerant disregard, but pigs, wheelbarrows, piles of stones by the roadside, perambulators in a village street, gates painted too aggressively white, and sometimes, but not always, the newer kind of beehives, turned him aside from his tracks in vivid imitation of the zigzag course of forked lightning. If a pheasant rose noisily from the other side of a hedgerow the Brogue would spring into the air at the same moment, but this may have been due to a desire to be companionable. The Mullet family contradicted the widely prevalent report that the horse was a confirmed crib-biter.

It was about the third week in May that Mrs. Mullet, relict of the late Sylvester Mullet, and mother of Toby and a bunch of daughters, assailed Clovis Sangrail on the outskirts of the village with a breathless catalogue of local happenings.

"You know our new neighbour, Mr. Penricarde?" she vociferated; "awfully rich, owns tin mines in Cornwall, middle-aged and rather quiet. He's taken the Red House on a long lease and spent a lot of money on alterations and improvements. Well, Toby's sold him the Brogue!"

Clovis spent a moment or two in assimilating the astonishing news; then he broke out into unstinted congratulation. If he had belonged to a more emotional race he would probably have kissed Mrs. Mullet.

"How wonderful lucky to have pulled it off at last! Now you can buy a decent animal. I've always said that Toby was clever. Ever so many congratulations."

"Don't congratulate me. It's the most unfortunate thing that could have happened!" said Mrs. Mullet dramatically.

Clovis stared at her in amazement.

"Mr. Penricarde," said Mrs. Mullet, sinking her voice to what she imagined to be an impressive whisper, though it rather resembled a hoarse, excited squeak, "Mr. Penricarde has just begun to pay attentions to Jessie. Slight at first, but now unmistakable. I was a fool not to have seen it sooner. Yesterday, at the Rectory garden party, he asked her what her favourite flowers were, and she told him carnations, and to-day a whole stack of carnations has arrived, clove and malmaison and lovely dark red ones, regular exhibition blooms, and a box of chocolates that he must have got on purpose from London. And he's asked her to go round the links with him to-morrow. And now, just at this critical moment, Toby has sold him that animal. It's a calamity!"

"But you've been trying to get the horse off your hands for years," said Clovis.

"I've got a houseful of daughters," said Mrs. Mullet, "and I've been trying—well, not to get them off my hands, of course, but a husband or two wouldn't be amiss among the lot of them; there are six of them, you know."

"I don't know," said Clovis, "I've never counted, but I expect you're right as to the number; mothers generally know these things."

"And now," continued Mrs. Mullet, in her tragic whisper, "when there's a rich husband-in-prospect imminent on the horizon Toby goes and sells him that miserable animal. It will probably kill him if he tries to ride it; anyway it will kill any affection he might have felt towards any member of our family. What is to be done? We can't very well ask to have the horse back; you see, we praised it up like anything when we thought there was a chance of his buying it, and said it was just the animal to suit him."

"Couldn't you steal it out of his stable and send it to grass at some farm miles away?" suggested Clovis; "write 'Votes for Women' on the stable door, and the thing would pass for a Suffragette outrage. No one who knew the horse could possibly suspect you of wanting to get it back again."

"Every newspaper in the country would ring with the affair," said Mrs. Mullet; "can't you imagine the headline, 'Valuable Hunter Stolen by Suffragettes'? The police would scour the countryside till they found the animal."

"Well, Jessie must try and get it back from Penricarde on the plea that it's an old favourite. She can say it was only sold because the stable had to be pulled down under the terms of an old repairing lease, and that now it has been arranged that the stable is to stand for a couple of years longer."

"It sounds a queer proceeding to ask for a horse back when you've just sold him," said Mrs. Mullet, "but something must be done, and done at once. The man is not used to horses, and I believe I told him it was as quiet as a lamb. After all, lambs go kicking and twisting about as if they were demented, don't they?"

"The lamb has an entirely unmerited character for sedateness," agreed Clovis.

Jessie came back from the golf links next day in a state of mingled elation and concern.

"It's all right about the proposal," she announced; "he came out with it at the sixth hole. I said I must have time to think it over. I accepted him at the seventh."

"My dear," said her mother, "I think a little more maidenly reserve and hesitation would have been advisable, as you've known him so short a time. You might have waited till the ninth hole."

"The seventh is a very long hole," said Jessie; "besides, the tension was putting us both off our game. By the time we'd got to the ninth hole we'd settled lots of things. The honeymoon is to be spent in Corsica, with perhaps a flying visit to Naples if we feel like it, and a week in London to wind up with. Two of his nieces are to be asked to be bridesmaids, so with our lot there will be seven, which is rather a lucky number. You are to wear your pearl grey, with any amount of Honiton lace jabbed into it. By the way, he's coming over this evening to ask your consent to the whole affair. So far all's well, but about the Brogue it's a different matter. I told him the legend about the stable, and how keen we were about buying the horse back, but he seems equally keen on keeping it. He said he must have horse exercise now that he's living in the country, and he's going to start riding to-morrow. He's ridden a few times in the Row on an animal that was accustomed to carry octogenarians and people undergoing rest cures, and that's about all his experience in the saddle—oh, and he rode a pony once in Norfolk, when he was fifteen and the pony twenty-four; and to-morrow he's going to ride the Brogue! I shall be a widow before I'm married, and I do so want to see what Corsica's like; it looks so silly on the map."

Clovis was sent for in haste, and the developments of the situation put before him.

"Nobody can ride that animal with any safety," said Mrs. Mullet, "except Toby, and he knows by long experience what it is going to shy at, and manages to swerve at the same time."

"I did hint to Mr. Penricarde—to Vincent, I should say—that the Brogue didn't like white gates," said Jessie.

"White gates!" exclaimed Mrs. Mullet; "did you mention what effect a pig has on him? He'll have to go past Lockyer's farm to get to the high road, and there's sure to be a pig or two grunting about in the lane."

"He's taken rather a dislike to turkeys lately," said Toby.

"It's obvious that Penricarde mustn't be allowed to go out on that animal," said Clovis, "at least not till Jessie has married him, and tired of him. I tell you what: ask him to a picnic to-morrow, starting at an early hour; he's not the sort to go out for a ride before breakfast. The day after I'll get the rector to drive him over to Crowleigh before lunch, to see the new cottage hospital they're building there. The Brogue will be standing idle in the stable and Toby can offer to exercise it; then it can pick up a stone or something of the sort and go conveniently lame. If you hurry on the wedding a bit the lameness fiction can be kept up till the ceremony is safely over."

Mrs. Mullet belonged to an emotional race, and she kissed Clovis.

It was nobody's fault that the rain came down in torrents the next morning, making a picnic a fantastic impossibility. It was also nobody's fault, but sheer ill-luck, that the weather cleared up sufficiently in the afternoon to tempt Mr. Penricarde to make his first essay with the Brogue. They did not get as far as the pigs at Lockyer's farm ; the rectory gate was painted a dull unobtrusive green, but it had been white a year or two ago, and the Brogue never forgot that he had been in the habit of making a violent curtsey, a back-pedal and a swerve at this particular point of the road. Subsequently, there being apparently no further call on his services, he broke his way into the rectory orchard, where he found a hen turkey in a coop ; later visitors to the orchard found the coop almost intact, but very little left of the turkey.

Mr. Penricarde, a little stunned and shaken, and suffering from a bruised knee and some minor damages, good-naturedly ascribed the accident to his own inexperience with horses and country roads, and allowed Jessie to nurse him back into complete recovery and golf-fitness within something less than a week.

In the list of wedding presents which the local newspaper published a fortnight or so later appeared the following item :

" Brown saddle-horse, 'The Brogue,' bridegroom's gift to bride."

" Which shows," said Toby Mullet, " that he knew nothing."

" Or else," said Clovis, " that he has a very pleasing wit."

THE HEN

"DORA BITTHOLZ is coming on Thursday," said Mrs. Sangrail.

"This next Thursday?" asked Clovis.

His mother nodded.

"You've rather done it, haven't you?" he chuckled; "Jane Martlet has only been here five days, and she never stays less than a fortnight, even when she's asked definitely for a week. You'll never get her out of the house by Thursday."

"Why should I?" asked Mrs. Sangrail; "she and Dora are good friends, aren't they? They used to be, as far as I remember."

"They used to be; that's what makes them all the more bitter now. Each feels that she has nursed a viper in her bosom. Nothing fans the flame of human resentment so much as the discovery that one's bosom has been utilized as a snake sanatorium."

"But what has happened? Has some one been making mischief?"

"Not exactly," said Clovis; "a hen came between them."

"A hen? What hen?"

"It was a bronze Leghorn or some such exotic breed, and Dora sold it to Jane at a rather exotic price. They both go in for prize poultry, you know, and Jane thought she was going to get her money back in a large family of pedigree chickens. The bird turned out to be an abstainer from the egg habit, and I'm told that the letters which passed between the two women were a revelation as to how much invective could be got on to a sheet of notepaper."

"How ridiculous!" said Mrs. Sangrail. "Couldn't some of their friends compose the quarrel?"

"People tried," said Clovis, "but it must have been rather like composing the storm music of the 'Fliegende Holländer.' Jane was willing to take back some of her most libellous remarks if Dora would take back the hen, but Dora said that would be owning herself in the wrong, and you know she'd as soon think of owning slum property in Whitechapel as do that."

"It's a most awkward situation," said Mrs. Sangrail. "Do you suppose they won't speak to one another?"

"On the contrary, the difficulty will be to get them to leave off. Their remarks on each other's conduct and character have hitherto been governed by the fact that only four ounces of plain speaking can be sent through the post for a penny."

"I can't put Dora off," said Mrs. Sangrail. "I've already postponed her visit once, and nothing short of a miracle would make Jane leave before her self-allotted fortnight is over."

"Miracles are rather in my line," said Clovis. "I don't pretend to be very hopeful in this case, but I'll do my best."

"As long as you don't drag me into it——" stipulated his mother.

. . .

"Servants are a bit of a nuisance," muttered Clovis, as he sat in the smoking-room after lunch, talking fitfully to Jane Martlet in the intervals of putting together the materials of a cocktail, which he had irreverently patented under the name of an Ella Wheeler Wilcox. It was partly compounded of old brandy and partly of curaçoa ; there were other ingredients, but they were never indiscriminately revealed.

"Servants a nuisance!" exclaimed Jane, bounding into the topic with the exuberant plunge of a hunter when it leaves the high road and feels turf under its hoofs ; "I should think they were! The trouble I've had in getting suited this year you would hardly believe. But I don't see what you have to complain of—your mother is so wonderfully lucky in her servants. Sturridge, for instance—he's been with you for years, and I'm sure he's a paragon as butlers go."

"That's just the trouble," said Clovis. "It's when servants have been with you for years that they become a really serious nuisance. The 'here to-day and gone to-morrow' sort don't matter—you've simply got to replace them ; it's the stayers and the paragons that are the real worry."

"But if they give satisfaction——"

"That doesn't prevent them from giving trouble. Now, you've mentioned Sturridge—it was Sturridge I was particularly thinking of when I made the observation about servants being a nuisance."

"The excellent Sturridge a nuisance! I can't believe it."

"I know he's excellent, and we just couldn't get along without him ; he's the one reliable element in this rather haphazard household. But his very orderliness has had an effect on him. Have you ever considered what it must be like to go on unceasingly doing the correct thing in the correct manner in the same surroundings for the greater part of a lifetime? To know and ordain and superintend exactly what silver and glass and table linen shall be used and set out on what occasions, to have cellar and pantry and plate-cupboard under a minutely devised and undeviating administration, to be noiseless, impalpable, omnipresent, and, as far as your own department is concerned, omniscient?"

"I should go mad," said Jane with conviction.

"Exactly," said Clovis thoughtfully, swallowing his completed Ella Wheeler Wilcox.

"But Sturridge hasn't gone mad," said Jane with a flutter of inquiry in her voice.

"On most points he's thoroughly sane and reliable," said Clovis, "but at times he is subject to the most obstinate delusions, and on those occasions he becomes not merely a nuisance but a decided embarrassment."

"What sort of delusions?"

"Unfortunately they usually centre round one of the guests of the house party, and that is where the awkwardness comes in. For instance, he took it into his head that Matilda Sheringham was the Prophet Elijah, and as all that he remembered about Elijah's history was the episode of the ravens in the wilderness he absolutely declined to interfere with what he imagined to be Matilda's private catering arrangements, wouldn't allow any tea to be sent up to her in the morning, and if he was waiting at table he passed her over altogether in handing round the dishes."

"How very unpleasant. Whatever did you do about it?"

"Oh, Matilda got fed, after a fashion, but it was judged to be best for her to cut her visit short. It was really the only thing to be done," said Clovis with some emphasis.

"I shouldn't have done that," said Jane, "I should

have humoured him in some way. I certainly shouldn't have gone away."

Clovis frowned.

"It is not always wise to humour people when they get these ideas into their heads. There's no knowing to what lengths they may go if you encourage them."

"You don't mean to say he might be dangerous, do you?" asked Jane with some anxiety.

"One can never be certain," said Clovis; "now and then he gets some idea about a guest which *might* take an unfortunate turn. That is precisely what is worrying me at the present moment."

"What, has he taken a fancy about some one here now?" asked Jane excitedly; "how thrilling! Do tell me who it is."

"You," said Clovis briefly.

"Me?"

Clovis nodded.

"Who on earth does he think I am?"

"Queen Anne," was the unexpected answer.

"Queen Anne! What an idea. But, anyhow, there's nothing dangerous about her; she's such a colourless personality."

"What does posterity chiefly say about Queen Anne?" asked Clovis rather sternly.

"The only thing that I can remember about her," said Jane, "is the saying 'Queen Anne's dead.'"

"Exactly," said Clovis, staring at the glass that had held the Ella Wheeler Wilcox, "dead."

"Do you mean he takes me for the ghost of Queen Anne?" asked Jane.

"Ghost? Dear no. No one ever heard of a ghost that came down to breakfast and ate kidneys and toast and honey with a healthy appetite. No, it's the fact of you being so very much alive and flourishing that perplexes and annoys him. All his life he has been accustomed to look on Queen Anne as the personification of everything that is dead and done with, 'as dead as Queen Anne,' you know ; and now he has to fill your glass at lunch and dinner and listen to your accounts of the gay time you had at the Dublin Horse Show, and naturally he feels that something's very wrong with you."

"But he wouldn't be downright hostile to me on that account, would he ?" Jane asked anxiously.

"I didn't get really alarmed about it till lunch to-day," said Clovis ; "I caught him glowering at you with a very sinister look and muttering : 'Ought to be dead long ago, she ought, and some one should see to it.' That's why I mentioned the matter to you."

"This is awful," said Jane ; "your mother must be told about it at once."

"My mother mustn't hear a word about it," said Clovis earnestly ; "it would upset her dreadfully. She relies on Sturridge for everything."

"But he might kill me at any moment," protested Jane.

"Not at any moment ; he's busy with the silver all the afternoon."

"You'll have to keep a sharp look-out all the time and be on your guard to frustrate any murderous attack," said Jane, adding in a tone of weak obstinacy : "It's a dreadful situation to be in, with a mad butler dangling over you like the sword of What's-his-name, but I'm certainly not going to cut my visit short."

Clovis swore horribly under his breath ; the miracle was an obvious misfire.

It was in the hall the next morning after a late

breakfast that Clovis had his final inspiration as he stood engaged in coaxing rust spots from an old putter.

"Where is Miss Martlet?" he asked the butler, who was at that moment crossing the hall.

"Writing letters in the morning-room, sir," said Sturridge, announcing a fact of which his questioner was already aware.

"She wants to copy the inscription on that old basket-hilted sabre," said Clovis, pointing to a venerable weapon hanging on the wall. "I wish you'd take it to her; my hands are all over oil. Take it without the sheath, it will be less trouble."

The butler drew the blade, still keen and bright in its well-cared for old age, and carried it into the morning-room. There was a door near the writing-table leading to a back stairway; Jane vanished through it with such lightning rapidity that the butler doubted whether she had seen him come in. Half an hour later Clovis was driving her and her hastily-packed luggage to the station.

"Mother will be awfully vexed when she comes back from her ride and finds you have gone," he observed to the departing guest, "but I'll make up some story about an urgent wire having called you away. It wouldn't do to alarm her unnecessarily about Sturridge."

Jane sniffed slightly at Clovis' ideas of unnecessary alarm, and was almost rude to the young man who came round with thoughtful inquiries as to luncheon-baskets.

The miracle lost some of its usefulness from the fact that Dora wrote the same day postponing the date of her visit, but, at any rate, Clovis holds the record as the only human being who ever hustled Jane Martlet out of the time-table of her migrations.

THE OPEN WINDOW

"MY aunt will be down presently, Mr. Nuttel," said a very self-possessed young lady of fifteen; "in the meantime you must try and put up with me."

Framton Nuttel endeavoured to say the correct something which should duly flatter the niece of the moment without unduly discounting the aunt that was to come. Privately he doubted more than ever whether these formal visits on a succession of total strangers would do much towards helping the nerve cure which he was supposed to be undergoing.

"I know how it will be," his sister had said when he was preparing to migrate to this rural retreat; "you will bury yourself down there and not speak to a living soul, and your nerves will be worse than ever from moping. I shall just give you letters of introduction to all the people I know there. Some of them, as far as I can remember, were quite nice."

Framton wondered whether Mrs. Sappleton, the lady to whom he was presenting one of the letters of introduction, came into the nice division.

"Do you know many of the people round here?" asked the niece, when she judged that they had had sufficient silent communion.

"Hardly a soul," said Framton. "My sister was was staying here, at the rectory, you know, some four years ago, and she gave me letters of introduction to some of the people here."

He made the last statement in a tone of distinct regret.

"Then you know practically nothing about my aunt?" pursued the self-possessed young lady.

"Only her name and address," admitted the caller. He was wondering whether Mrs. Sappleton was in the married or widowed state. An undefinable something about the room seemed to suggest masculine habitation.

"Her great tragedy happened just three years ago," said the child; "that would be since your sister's time."

"Her tragedy?" asked Framton; somehow in this restful country spot tragedies seemed out of place.

"You may wonder why we keep that window wide open on an October afternoon," said the niece, indicating a large French window that opened on to a lawn.

"It is quite warm for the time of the year," said Framton; "but has that window got anything to do with the tragedy?"

"Out through that window, three years ago to a day, her husband and her two young brothers went off for their day's shooting. They never came back. In crossing the moor to their favourite snipe-shooting ground they were all three engulfed in a treacherous piece of bog. It had been that dreadful wet summer, you know, and places that were safe in other years gave way suddenly without warning. Their bodies were never recovered. That was the dreadful part of it." Here the child's voice lost its self-possessed note and became falteringly human. "Poor aunt always thinks that they will come back some day, they and the little brown spaniel that was lost with them, and walk in at that window just as they used to do. That is why the window is kept open every evening till it is quite dusk. Poor dear aunt, she has often told me how they went out, her husband with his white waterproof coat over his arm, and Ronnie, her youngest brother, singing 'Bertie, why do you bound?' as he always did to tease her, because she said it got on her nerves. Do you know, sometimes on still, quiet evenings like this, I almost get a creepy feeling that they will all walk in through that window——"

She broke off with a little shudder. It was a relief to Framton when the aunt bustled into the room with a whirl of apologies for being late in making her appearance.

"I hope Vera has been amusing you?" she said.

"She has been very interesting," said Framton.

"I hope you don't mind the open windpw," said Mrs. Sappleton briskly; "my husband and brothers will be home directly from shooting, and they always come in this way. They've been out for snipe in the marshes to-day, so they'll make a fine mess over my poor carpets. So like you men-folk, isn't it?"

She rattled on cheerfully about the shooting and the scarcity of birds, and the prospects for duck in the winter. To Framton it was all purely horrible. He made a desperate but only partially successful effort to turn the talk on to a less ghastly topic; he was conscious that his hostess was giving him only a fragment of her attention, and her eyes were constantly straying past him to the open window and the lawn beyond. It was certainly an unfortunate coincidence that he should have paid his visit on this tragic anniversary.

"The doctors agree in ordering me complete rest, an absence of mental excitement, and avoidance of anything in the nature of violent physical exercise," announced Framton, who laboured under the tolerably wide-spread delusion that total strangers and chance acquaintances are hungry for the least detail of one's ailments and infirmities, their cause and cure. "On the matter of diet they are not so much in agreement," he continued.

"No?" said Mrs. Sappleton, in a voice which only replaced a yawn at the last moment. Then she suddenly brightened into alert attention—but not to what Framton was saying.

"Here they are at last!" she cried. "Just in time for tea, and don't they look as if they were muddy up to the eyes!"

Framton shivered slightly and turned towards the niece with a look intended to convey sympathetic comprehension. The child was staring out through the open window with dazed horror in her eyes. In a chill shock of nameless fear Framton swung round in his seat and looked in the same direction.

In the deepening twilight three figures were walking across the lawn towards the window; they all carried guns under their arms, and one of them was additionally burdened with a white coat hung over his shoulders. A tired brown spaniel kept close at their heels. Noiselessly they neared the house, and then a hoarse young voice chanted out of the dusk: "I said, Bertie, why do you bound?"

Framton grabbed wildly at his stick and hat; the hall-door, the gravel-drive, and the front gate were dimly-noted stages in his headlong retreat. A cyclist coming along the road had to run into the hedge to avoid imminent collision.

" Here we are, my dear," said the bearer of the white mackintosh, coming in through the window; " fairly muddy, but most of it's dry. Who was that who bolted out as we came up?"

" A most extraordinary man, a Mr. Nuttel," said Mrs. Sappleton; " could only talk about his illnesses, and dashed off without a word of good-bye or apology when you arrived. One would think he had seen a ghost."

" I expect it was the spaniel," said the niece calmly; " he told me he had a horror of dogs. He was once hunted into a cemetery somewhere on the banks of the Ganges by a pack of pariah dogs, and had to spend the night in a newly dug grave with the creatures snarling and grinning and foaming just above him. Enough to make anyone lose their nerve."

Romance at short notice was her speciality.

THE TREASURE-SHIP

THE great galleon lay in semi-retirement under the sand and weed and water of the northern bay where the fortune of war and weather had long ago ensconced it. Three and a quarter centuries had passed since the day when it had taken the high seas as an important unit of a fighting squadron—precisely which squadron the learned were not agreed. The galleon had brought nothing into the world, but it had, according to tradition and report, taken much out of it. But how much? There again the learned were in disagreement. Some were as generous in their estimate as an income-tax assessor, others applied a species of higher criticism to the submerged treasure chests, and debased their contents to the currency of goblin gold. Of the former school was Lulu, Duchess of Dulverton.

The Duchess was not only a believer in the existence of a sunken treasure of alluring proportions; she also believed that she knew of a method by which the said treasure might be precisely located and cheaply disembedded. An aunt on her mother's side of the family had been Maid of Honour at the Court of Monaco, and had taken a respectful interest in the deep-sea researches in which the Throne of that country, impatient perhaps of its terrestrial restrictions, was wont to immerse itself. It was through the instrumentality of this relative that the Duchess learned of an invention, perfected and very nearly patented by a Monegaskan savant, by means of which the home-life of the Mediterranean sardine might be studied at a depth of many fathoms in a cold white light of more than ball-room brilliancy. Implicated in this invention (and, in the Duchess's eyes, the most attractive part of it) was an electric suction dredge, specially designed for dragging to the surface such objects of interest and value as might be found in the more accessible levels of the ocean-bed. The rights of the invention were to be acquired for a matter of eighteen hundred francs, and the apparatus for a few thousand more. The Duchess of Dulverton was rich, as the world counted wealth; she nursed the hope of being one day rich at her own computation. Companies had been formed and efforts had been made again and again during the course of three centuries to probe for the alleged treasures of the interesting galleon; with the aid of this invention she considered that she might go to work on the wreck privately and independently. After all, one of her ancestors on her mother's side was descended from Medina Sidonia, so she was of opinion that she had as much right to the treasure as anyone. She acquired the invention and bought the apparatus.

Among other family ties and encumbrances, Lulu possessed a nephew, Vasco Honiton, a young gentleman who was blessed with a small income and a large circle of relatives, and lived impartially and precariously on both. The name Vasco had been given him possibly in the hope that he might live up to its adventurous tradition, but he limited himself strictly to the home industry of adventurer, preferring to exploit the assured rather than to explore the unknown. Lulu's intercourse with him had been restricted of recent years to the negative processes of being out of town when he called on her, and short of money when he wrote to her. Now, however, she bethought herself of his eminent suitability for the direction of a treasure-seeking experiment; if anyone could extract gold from an unpromising situation it would certainly be Vasco—of course, under the necessary safeguards in the way of supervision. Where money was in question Vasco's conscience was liable to fits of obstinate silence.

Somewhere on the west coast of Ireland the Dulverton property included a few acres of shingle, rock, and heather, too barren to support even an agrarian outrage, but embracing a small and fairly deep bay where the lobster yield was good in most seasons. There was a bleak little house on the property, and for those who liked lobsters and solitude, and were able to accept an Irish cook's ideas as to what might be perpetrated in the name of mayonnaise, Innisgluther was a tolerable exile during the summer months. Lulu seldom went there herself, but she lent the house lavishly to friends and relations. She put it now at Vasco's disposal.

"It will be the very place to practise and experiment with the salvage apparatus," she said; "the bay is quite deep in places, and you will be able to test everything thoroughly before starting on the treasure hunt."

In less than three weeks Vasco turned up in town to report progress.

"The apparatus works beautifully," he informed his aunt; "the deeper one got the clearer everything grew. We found something in the way of a sunken wreck to operate on, too!"

"A wreck in Innisgluther Bay!" exclaimed Lulu.

"A submerged motor-boat, the *Sub-Rosa*," said Vasco.

"No! really?" said Lulu; "poor Billy Yuttley's boat. I remember it went down somewhere off that coast some three years ago. His body was washed ashore at the Point. People said at the time that the boat was capsized intentionally—a case of suicide, you know. People always say that sort of thing when anything tragic happens."

"In this case they were right," said Vasco.

"What do you mean?" asked the Duchess hurriedly. "What makes you think so?"

"I know," said Vasco simply.

"Know? How can you know? How can anyone know? The thing happened three years ago."

"In a locker of the *Sub-Rosa* I found a watertight strong-box. It contained papers." Vasco paused with dramatic effect and searched for a moment in the inner breast-pocket of his coat. He drew out a folded slip of paper. The Duchess snatched at it in almost indecent haste and moved appreciably nearer the fireplace.

"Was this in the *Sub-Rosa's* strong-box?" she asked.

"Oh no," said Vasco carelessly, "that is a list of the well-known people who would be involved in a very disagreeable scandal if the *Sub-Rosa's* papers were made public. I've put you at the head of it, otherwise it follows alphabetical order."

The Duchess gazed helplessly at the string of names, which seemed for the moment to include nearly every one she knew. As a matter of fact, her own name at the head of the list exercised an almost paralysing effect on her thinking faculties.

"Of course you have destroyed the papers?" she asked, when she had somewhat recovered herself. She was conscious that she made the remark with an entire lack of conviction.

Vasco shook his head.

"But you should have," said Lulu angrily; "if, as you say, they are highly compromising——"

"Oh, they are, I assure you of that," interposed the young man.

"Then you should put them out of harm's way at once. Supposing anything should leak out, think of all these poor, unfortunate people who would be involved in the disclosures," and Lulu tapped the list with an agitated gesture.

"Unfortunate, perhaps, but not poor," corrected Vasco; "if you read the list carefully you'll notice that I haven't troubled to include anyone whose financial standing isn't above question."

Lulu glared at her nephew for some moments in silence. Then she asked hoarsely: "What are you going to do?"

"Nothing—for the remainder of my life," he answered meaningly. "A little hunting, perhaps," he continued, "and I shall have a villa at Florence. The Villa Sub-Rosa would sound rather quaint and picturesque, don't you think, and quite a lot of people would be able to attach a meaning to the name. And I suppose I must have a hobby; I shall probably collect Raeburns."

Lulu's relative, who lived at the Court of Monaco, got quite a snappish answer when she wrote recommending some further invention in the realm of marine research.

THE COBWEB

THE farmhouse kitchen probably stood where it did as a matter of accident or haphazard choice; yet its situation might have been planned by a master-strategist in farmhouse architecture. Dairy and poultry-yard, and herb garden, and all the busy places of the farm seemed to lead by easy access into its wide flagged haven, where there was room for everything and where muddy boots left traces that were easily swept away. And yet, for all that it stood so well in the centre of human bustle, its long, latticed window, with the wide window-seat, built into an embrasure beyond the huge fireplace, looked out on a wild spreading view of hill and heather and wooded combe. The window nook made almost a little room it itself, quite the pleasantest room in the farm as far as situation and capabilities went. Young Mrs. Ladbruk, whose husband had just come into the farm by way of inheritance, cast covetous eyes on this snug corner, and her fingers itched to make it bright and cosy with chintz curtains and bowls of flowers, and a shelf or two of old china. The musty farm parlour, looking out to a prim, cheerless garden imprisoned within high, blank walls, was not a room that lent itself readily either to comfort or decoration.

"When we are more settled I shall work wonders in the way of making the kitchen habitable," said the young woman to her occasional visitors. There was an unspoken wish in those words, a wish which was unconfessed as well as unspoken. Emma Ladbruk was the mistress of the farm ; jointly with her husband she might have her say, and to a certain extent her way, in ordering its affairs. But she was not mistress of the kitchen.

On one of the shelves of an old dresser, in company with chipped sauce-boats, pewter jugs, cheese-graters, and paid bills, rested a worn and ragged Bible, on whose front page was the record, in faded ink, of a baptism dated ninety-four years ago. " Martha Crale " was the name written on that yellow page. The yellow, wrinkled old dame who hobbled and muttered about the kitchen, looking like a dead autumn leaf which the winter winds still pushed hither and thither, had once been Martha Crale ; for seventy odd years she had been Martha Mountjoy. For longer than anyone could remember she had pattered to and fro between oven and wash-house and dairy, and out to chicken-run and garden, grumbling and muttering and scolding, but working unceasingly. Emma Ladbruk, of whose coming she took as little notice as she would of a bee wandering in at a window on a summer's day, used at first to watch her with a kind of frightened curiosity. She was so old and so much a part of the place, it was difficult to think of her exactly as a living thing. Old Shep, the white-nozzled, stiff-limbed collie, waiting for his time to die, seemed almost more human than the withered, dried-up old woman. He had been a riotous, roystering puppy, mad with the joy of life, when she was already a tottering, hobbling dame ; now he was just a blind, breathing carcase, nothing more, and she still worked with frail energy, still swept and baked and washed, fetched and carried. If there were something in these wise old dogs that did not perish utterly with death, Emma used to think to herself, what generations of ghost-dogs there must be out on those hills, that Martha had reared and fed and tended and spoken a last good-bye word to in that old kitchen. And what memories she must have of human generations that had passed away in her time. It was difficult for anyone, let alone a stranger like Emma, to get her to talk of the days that had been ; her shrill, quavering speech was of doors that had been left unfastened, pails that had got mislaid, calves whose feeding-time was overdue, and the various little faults and lapses that chequer a farmhouse routine. Now and again, when election time came round, she would unstore her recollections of the old names round which the fight had waged in the days gone by. There had been a Palmerston, that had been a name down Tiverton way ; Tiverton was not a far journey as the crow flies, but to Martha it was almost a foreign country. Later there had been Northcotes and Aclands, and many other newer names that she had forgotten ; the names changed, but it was always Libruls and Toories, Yellows and Blues. And they always quarrelled and shouted as to who was right and who was wrong. The one they quarrelled about most was a fine old gentleman with an angry face—she had seen his picture on the walls. She had seen it on the floor too, with a rotten apple squashed over it, for the farm had changed its politics from time to time. Martha had never been on one side or the other ; none of "they" had ever done the farm a stroke of good. Such was her sweeping verdict, given with all a peasant's distrust of the outside world.

When the half-frightened curiosity had somewhat

faded away, Emma Ladbruk was uncomfortably conscious of another feeling towards the old woman. She was a quaint old tradition, lingering about the place, she was part and parcel of the farm itself, she was something at once pathetic and picturesque—but she was dreadfully in the way. Emma had come to the farm full of plans for little reforms and improvements, in part the result of training in the newest ways and methods, in part the outcome of her own ideas and fancies. Reforms in the kitchen region, if those deaf old ears could have been induced to give them even a hearing, would have met with short shrift and scornful rejection, and the kitchen region spread over the zone of dairy and market business and half the work of the household. Emma, with the latest science of dead-poultry dressing at her fingertips, sat by, an unheeded watcher, while old Martha trussed the chickens for the market-stall as she had trussed them for nearly four-score years—all leg and no breast. And the hundred hints anent effective cleaning and labour-lightening and the things that make for wholesomeness which the young woman was ready to impart or to put into action dropped away into nothingness before that wan, muttering, unheeding presence. Above all, the coveted window corner, that was to be a dainty, cheerful oasis in the gaunt old kitchen, stood now choked and lumbered with a litter of odds and ends that Emma, for all her nominal authority, would not have dared or cared to displace ; over them seemed to be spun the protection of something that was like a human cobweb. Decidedly Martha was in the way. It would have been an unworthy meanness to have wished to see the span of that brave old life shortened by a few paltry months, but as the days sped by Emma was conscious that the wish was there, disowned though it might be, lurking at the back of her mind.

She felt the meanness of the wish come over her with a qualm of self-reproach one day when she came into the kitchen and found an unaccustomed state of things in that usually busy quarter. Old Martha was not working. A basket of corn was on the floor by her side, and out in the yard the poultry were beginning to clamour a protest of overdue feeding-time. But Martha sat huddled in a shrunken bunch on the window seat, looking out with her dim old eyes as though she saw something stranger than the autumn landscape.

"Is anything the matter, Martha?" asked the young woman.

"'Tis death, 'tis death a-coming," answered the quavering voice; "I knew 'twere coming. I knew it. 'Tweren't for nothing that old Shep's been howling all morning. An' last night I heard the screech-owl give the death-cry, and there were something white as run across the yard yesterday; 'tweren't a cat nor a stoat, 'twere something. The fowls knew 'twere something; they all drew off to one side. Ay, there's been warnings. I knew it were a-coming."

The young woman's eyes clouded with pity. The old thing sitting there so white and shrunken had once been a merry, noisy child, playing about in lanes and hay-lofts and farmhouse garrets; that had been eighty odd years ago, and now she was just a frail old body cowering under the approaching chill of the death that was coming at last to take her. It was not probable that much could be done for her, but Emma hastened away to get assistance and counsel. Her husband, she knew, was down at a tree-felling some little distance off, but she might find some other intelligent soul who knew the old woman better than she did. The farm, she soon found out, had that faculty common to farmyards of swallowing up and losing its human population. The poultry followed her in interested fashion, and swine grunted interrogations at her from behind the bars of their styes, but barnyard and rickyard, orchard and stables and dairy, gave no reward to her search. Then, as she retraced her steps towards the kitchen, she came suddenly on her cousin, young Mr. Jim, as every one called him, who divided his time between amateur horse-dealing, rabbit-shooting, and flirting with the farm maids.

"I'm afraid old Martha is dying," said Emma. Jim was not the sort of person to whom one had to break news gently.

"Nonsense," he said; "Martha means to live to a hundred. She told me so, and she'll do it."

"She may be actually dying at this moment, or it may just be the beginning of the break-up," persisted Emma, with a feeling of contempt for the slowness and dullness of the young man.

A grin spread over his good-natured features.

"It don't look like it," he said, nodding towards the yard. Emma turned to catch the meaning of his remark. Old Martha stood in the middle of a mob of poultry scattering handfuls of grain around her. The turkey-cock, with the bronzed sheen of his feathers and the purple-red of his wattles, the gamecock with the glowing metallic lustre of his Eastern plumage, the hens, with their ochres and buffs and umbers and their scarlet combs, and the drakes, with their bottle-green heads, made a medley of rich colour, in the centre of which the old woman looked like a withered stalk standing amid the riotous growth of gaily-hued flowers. But she threw the grain deftly amid the wilderness of beaks, and her quavering voice carried as far as the two people who were watching her. She was still harping on the theme of death coming to the farm.

"I knew 'twere a-coming. There's been signs an' warnings."

"Who's dead, then, old Mother?" called out the young man.

"'Tis young Mister Ladbruk," she shrilled back; "they've just a-carried his body in. Run out of the way of a tree that was coming down an' ran hisself on to an iron post. Dead when they picked un up. Aye, I knew 'twere coming."

And she turned to fling a handful of barley at a belated group of guinea-fowl that came racing toward her.

. . . . .

The farm was a family property, and passed to the rabbit-shooting cousin as the next-of-kin. Emma Ladbruk drifted out of its history as a bee that had wandered in at an open window might flit its way out again. On a cold grey morning she stood waiting with her boxes already stowed in the farm cart, till the last of the market produce should be ready, for the train she was to catch was of less importance than the chickens and butter and eggs that were to be offered for sale. From where she stood she could see an angle of the long latticed window that was to have been cosy with curtains and gay with bowls of flowers. Into her mind came the thought that for months, perhaps for years, long after she had been utterly forgotten, a white, unheeding face would be seen peering out through those latticed panes, and a weak muttering voice would be heard quavering up and down those flagged passages. She made her way to a narrow barred casement that opened into the farm larder. Old Martha was standing at a table trussing a pair of chickens for the market stall as she had trussed them for nearly fourscore years.

THE LULL

"I'VE asked Latimer Springfield to spend Sunday with us and stop the night," announced Mrs. Durmot at the breakfast-table.

"I thought he was in the throes of an election," remarked her husband.

"Exactly; the poll is on Wednesday, and the poor man will have worked himself to a shadow by that time. Imagine what electioneering must be like in this awful soaking rain, going along slushy country roads and speaking to damp audiences in draughty schoolrooms, day after day for a fortnight. He'll have to put in an appearance at some place of worship on Sunday morning, and he can come to us immediately afterwards and have a thorough respite from everything connected with politics. I won't let him even think of them. I've had the picture of Cromwell dissolving the Long Parliament taken down from the staircase, and even the potrait of Lord Rosebery's 'Ladas' removed from the smoking-room. And Vera," added Mrs. Durmot, turning to her sixteen-year-old niece, "be careful what colour ribbon you wear in your hair; not blue or yellow on any account; those are the rival party colours, and emerald green or orange would be almost as bad, with this Home Rule business to the fore."

"On state occasions I always wear a black ribbon in my hair," said Vera with crushing dignity.

Latimer Springfield was a rather cheerless, oldish young man, who went into politics somewhat in the spirit in which other people might go into half mourning. Without being an enthusiast, however, he was a fairly strenuous plodder, and Mrs. Durmot had been reasonably near the mark in asserting that he was working at high pressure over this election. The restful lull which his hostess enforced on him was decidedly welcome, and yet the nervous excitement of the contest had too great a hold on him to be totally banished.

"I know he's going to sit up half the night working up points for his final speeches," said Mrs. Durmot regretfully; "however, we've kept politics at arm's length all the afternoon and evening. More than that we cannot do."

"That remains to be seen," said Vera, but she said it to herself.

Latimer had scarcely shut his bedroom door before he was immersed in a sheaf of notes and pamphlets, while a fountain-pen and pocket-book were brought into play for the due marshalling of useful facts and discreet fictions. He had been at work for perhaps thirty-five minutes, and the house was seemingly consecrated to the healthy slumber of country life, when a stifled squealing and scuffling in the passage was followed by a loud tap at his door. Before he had time to answer, a much-encumbered Vera burst into the room with the question: "I say, can I leave these here?"

"These" were a small black pig and a lusty specimen of black-red gamecock.

Latimer was moderately fond of animals, and particularly interested in small livestock rearing from the economic point of view; in fact, one of the pamphlets on which he was at that moment engaged warmly advocated the further development of the pig and poultry industry in our rural districts; but he was pardonably unwilling to share even a commodious bedroom with samples of henroost and stye products.

"Wouldn't they be happier somewhere outside?" he asked, tactfully expressing his own preference in the matter in an apparent solicitude for theirs.

"There is no outside," said Vera impressively, "nothing but a waste of dark, swirling waters. The reservoir at Brinkley has burst."

"I didn't know there was a reservoir at Brinkley," said Latimer.

"Well, there isn't now, it's jolly well all over the place, and as we stand particularly low we're the centre of an inland sea just at present. You see the river has overflowed its banks as well."

"Good gracious! Have any lives been lost?"

"Heaps, I should say. The second housemaid has already identified three bodies that have floated past the billiard-room window as being the young man she's engaged to. Either she's engaged to a large assortment of the population round here or else she's very careless at identification. Of course it may be the same body coming round again and again in a swirl; I hadn't thought of that."

"But we ought to go out and do rescue work, oughtn't we?" said Latimer, with the instinct of a Parliamentary candidate for getting into the local limelight.

"We can't," said Vera decidedly, "we haven't any boats and we're cut off by a raging torrent from any human habitation. My aunt particularly hoped you would keep to your room and not add to the confusion, but she thought it would be so kind of you if you would take in Hartlepool's Wonder, the gamecock, you know, for the night. You see, there are eight other gamecocks, and they fight like furies if they get together, so we're putting one in each bedroom. The fowl-houses are all flooded out, you know. And then I thought perhaps you wouldn't mind taking in this wee piggie ; he's rather a little love, but he has a vile temper. He gets that from his mother—not that I like to say things against her when she's lying dead and drowned in her sty, poor thing. What he really wants is a man's firm hand to keep him in order. I'd try and grapple with him myself, only I've got my chow in my room, you know, and he goes for pigs wherever he finds them."

"Couldn't the pig go in the bathroom ?" asked Latimer faintly, wishing that he had taken up as determined a stand on the subject of bedroom swine as the chow had.

"The bathroom ?" Vera laughed shrilly. "It'll be full of Boy Scouts till morning if the hot water holds out."

"Boy Scouts ?"

"Yes, thirty of them came to rescue us while the water was only waist-high ; then it rose another three feet or so and we had to rescue them. We're giving them hot baths in batches and drying their clothes in the hot-air cupboard, but, of course, drenched clothes don't dry in a minute, and the corridor and staircase are beginning to look like a bit of coast scenery by Tuke. Two of the boys are wearing your Melton overcoat ; I hope you don't mind."

"It's a new overcoat," said Latimer, with every indication of minding dreadfully.

"You'll take every care of Hartlepool's Wonder, won't you?" said Vera. "His mother took three firsts at Birmingham, and he was second in the cockerel class last year at Gloucester. He'll probably roost on the rail at the bottom of your bed. I wonder if he'd feel more at home if some of his wives were up here with him? The hens are all in the pantry, and I think I could pick out Hartlepool Helen; she's his favourite."

Latimer showed a belated firmness on the subject of Hartlepool Helen, and Vera withdrew without pressing the point, having first settled the gamecock on his extemporized perch and taken an affectionate farewell of the pigling. Latimer undressed and got into bed with all due speed, judging that the pig would abate its inquisitorial restlessness once the light was turned out. As a substitute for a cosy, straw-bedded sty the room offered, at first inspection, few attractions, but the disconsolate animal suddenly discovered an appliance in which the most luxuriously contrived piggeries were notably deficient. The sharp edge of the underneath part of the bed was pitched at exactly the right elevation to permit the pigling to scrape himself ecstatically backwards and forwards, with an artistic humping of the back at the crucial moment and an accompanying gurgle of long-drawn delight. The gamecock, who may have fancied that he was being rocked in the branches of a pine-tree, bore the motion with greater fortitude than Latimer was able to command. A series of slaps directed at the pig's body were accepted more as an additional and pleasing irritant than as a criticism of conduct or a hint to desist;

evidently something more than a man's firm hand was needed to deal with the case. Latimer slipped out of bed in search of a weapon of dissuasion. There was sufficient light in the room to enable the pig to detect this manœuvre, and the vile temper, inherited from the drowned mother, found full play. Latimer bounded back into bed, and his conqueror, after a few threatening snorts and champings of its jaws, resumed its massage operations with renewed zeal. During the long wakeful hours which ensued Latimer tried to distract his mind from his own immediate troubles by dwelling with decent sympathy on the second housemaid's bereavement, but he found himself more often wondering how many Boy Scouts were sharing his Melton overcoat. The rôle of Saint Martin malgré lui was not one which appealed to him.

Towards dawn the pigling fell into a happy slumber, and Latimer might have followed its example, but at about the same time Stupor Hartlepooli gave a rousing crow, clattered down to the floor and forthwith commenced a spirited combat with his reflection in the wardrobe mirror. Remembering that the bird was more or less under his care Latimer performed Hague Tribunal offices by draping a bath-towel over the provocative mirror, but the ensuing peace was local and short-lived. The deflected energies of the gamecock found new outlet in a sudden and sustained attack on the sleeping and temporarily inoffensive pigling, and the duel which followed was desperate and embittered beyond any possibility of effective intervention. The feathered combatant had the advantage of being able, when hard pressed, to take refuge on the bed, and freely availed himself of this circumstance ; the pigling never quite succeeded in hurling himself on to the same eminence, but it was not from want of trying.

Neither side could claim any decisive success, and the struggle had been practically fought to a standstill by the time that the maid appeared with the early morning tea.

"Lor, sir," she exclaimed in undisguised astonishment, "do you want those animals in your room?"

Want!

The pigling, as though aware that it might have outstayed its welcome, dashed out at the door, and the gamecock followed it at a more dignified pace.

"If Miss Vera's dog sees that pig——!" exclaimed the maid, and hurried off to avert such a catastrophe.

A cold suspicion was stealing over Latimer's mind; he went to the window and drew up the blind. A light, drizzling rain was falling, but there was not the faintest trace of any inundation.

Some half-hour later he met Vera on the way to the breakfast-room.

"I should not like to think of you as a deliberate liar," he observed coldly, "but one occasionally has to do things one does not like."

"At any rate I kept your mind from dwelling on politics all the night," said Vera.

Which was, of course, perfectly true.

THE UNKINDEST BLOW

THE season of strikes seemed to have run itself to a standstill. Almost every trade and industry and calling in which a dislocation could possibly be engineered had indulged in that luxury. The last and least successful convulsion had been the strike of the World's Union of Zoological Garden attendants, who, pending the settlement of certain demands, refused to minister further to the wants of the animals committed to their charge or to allow any other keepers to take their place. In this case the threat of the Zoological Gardens authorities that if the men "came out" the animals should come out also had intensified and precipitated the crisis. This imminent prospect of the larger carnivores, to say nothing of rhinoceroses and bull bison, roaming at large and unfed in the heart of London, was not one which permitted of prolonged conferences. The Government of the day, which from its tendency to be a few hours behind the course of events had been nicknamed the Government of the afternoon, was obliged to intervene with promptitude and decision. A strong force of Bluejackets was despatched to Regent's Park to take over the temporarily abandoned duties of the strikers. Bluejackets were chosen in preference to land forces, partly on account of the traditional readiness of the British Navy to go anywhere and do anything, partly by reason of the familiarity of the average sailor with monkeys, parrots, and other tropical fauna, but chiefly at the urgent request of the First Lord of the Admiralty, who was keenly desirous of an opportunity for performing some personal act of unobtrusive public service within the province of his department.

"If he insists on feeding the infant jaguar himself, in defiance of its mother's wishes, there may be another by-election in the north," said one of his colleagues, with a hopeful inflection in his voice. "By-elections are not very desirable at present, but we must not be selfish."

As a matter of fact the strike collapsed peacefully without any outside intervention. The majority of the keepers had become so attached to their charges that they returned to work of their own accord.

And then the nation and the newspapers turned with a sense of relief to happier things. It seemed as if a new era of contentment was about to dawn. Everybody had struck who could possibly want to strike or who could possibly be cajoled or bullied into striking, whether they wanted to or not. The lighter and brighter side of life might now claim some attention. And conspicuous among the other topics that sprang into sudden prominence was the pending Falvertoon divorce suit.

The Duke of Falvertoon was one of those human *hors d'œuvres* that stimulate the public appetite for sensation without giving it much to feed on. As a mere child he had been precociously brilliant; he had declined the editorship of the *Anglian Review* at an age when most boys are content to have declined *mensa*, a table, and though he could not claim to have originated the Futurist movement in literature, his "Letters to a possible Grandson," written at the age of fourteen, had attracted considerable notice. In later days his brilliancy had been less conspicuously displayed. During a debate in the House of Lords on affairs in Morocco, at a moment when that country, for the fifth time in seven years, had brought half Europe to the verge of war, he had interpolated the remark "a little Moor and how much it is," but in spite of the encouraging reception accorded to this one political utterance he was never tempted to a further display in that direction. It began to be generally understood that he did not intend to supplement his numerous town and country residences by living overmuch in the public eye.

And then had come the unlooked-for tidings of the imminent proceedings for divorce. And such a divorce! There were cross-suits and allegations and counter-allegations, charges of cruelty and desertion, everything in fact that was necessary to make the case one of the most complicated and sensational of its kind. And the number of distinguished people involved or cited as witnesses not only embraced both political parties in the realm and several Colonial governors, but included an exotic contingent from France, Hungary, the United States of North America, and the Grand Duchy of Baden. Hotel accommodation of the more expensive sort began to experience a strain on its resources. "It will be quite like the Durbar without the elephants," exclaimed an enthusiastic lady who, to do her justice, had never seen a Durbar. The general feeling was one of thankfulness that the last of the strikes had been got over before the date fixed for the hearing of the great suit.

As a reaction from the season of gloom and industrial strife that had just passed away the agencies that purvey and stage-manage sensations laid themselves out to do their level best on this momentous occasion. Men who had made their reputations as special descriptive writers were mobilized from distant corners of Europe and the further side of the Atlantic in order to enrich with their pens the daily printed records of the case; one word-painter, who specialized in descriptions of how witnesses turn pale under cross-examination, was summoned hurriedly back from a famous and prolonged murder trial in Sicily, where indeed his talents were being decidedly wasted. Thumb-nail artists and expert kodak manipulators were retained at extravagant salaries, and special dress reporters were in high demand. An enterprising Paris firm of costume builders presented the defendant Duchess with three special creations, to be worn, marked, learned, and extensively reported at various critical stages of the trial; and as for the cinematograph agents, their industry and persistence was untiring. Films representing the Duke saying good-bye to his favourite canary on the eve of the trial were in readiness weeks before the event was due to take place; other films depicted the Duchess holding imaginary consultations with fictitious lawyers or making a light repast off specially advertised vegetarian sandwiches during a supposed luncheon interval. As far as human foresight and human enterprise could go nothing was lacking to make the trial a success.

Two days before the case was down for hearing the advance reporter of an important syndicate obtained an interview with the Duke for the purpose of gleaning some final grains of information concerning his Grace's personal arrangements during the trial.

"I suppose I may say this will be one of the biggest affairs of its kind during the lifetime of a generation," began the reporter as an excuse for the unsparing minuteness of detail that he was about to make quest for.

"I suppose so—if it comes off," said the Duke lazily.

"If?" queried the reporter, in a voice that was something between a gasp and a scream.

"The Duchess and I are both thinking of going on strike," said the Duke.

"Strike!"

The baleful word flashed out in all its old hideous familiarity. Was there to be no end to its recurrence?

"Do you mean," faltered the reporter, "that you are contemplating a mutual withdrawal of the charges?"

"Precisely," said the Duke.

"But think of the arrangements that have been made, the special reporting, the cinematographs, the catering for the distinguished foreign witnesses, the prepared music-hall allusions; think of all the money that has been sunk——"

"Exactly," said the Duke coldly, "the Duchess and I have realized that it is we who provide the material out of which this great far-reaching industry has been built up. Widespread employment will be given and enormous profits made during the duration of the case, and we, on whom all the stress and racket falls, will get—what? An unenviable notoriety and the privilege of paying heavy legal expenses whichever way the verdict goes. Hence our decision to strike. We don't wish to be reconciled ; we fully realize that it is a grave step to take, but unless we get some reasonable consideration out of this vast stream of wealth and industry that we have called into being we intend coming out of court and staying out. Good afternoon."

The news of this latest strike spread universal dismay. Its inaccessiblity to the ordinary methods of persuasion made it peculiarly formidable. If the Duke and Duchess persisted in being reconciled the Government could hardly be called on to interfere. Public opinion in the shape of social ostracism might be brought to bear on them, but that was as far as coercive measures could go. There was nothing for it but a conference, with powers to propose liberal terms. As it was, several of the foreign witnesses had already departed and others had telegraphed cancelling their hotel arrangements.

The conference, protracted, uncomfortable, and occasionally acrimonious, succeeded at last in arranging for a resumption of litigation, but it was a fruitless victory. The Duke, with a touch of his earlier precocity, died of premature decay a fortnight before the date fixed for the new trial.

THE ROMANCERS

IT was autumn in London, that blessed season between the harshness of winter and the insincerities of summer ; a trustful season when one buys bulbs and sees to the registration of one's vote, believing perpetually in spring and a change of Government.

Morton Crosby sat on a bench in a secluded corner of Hyde Park, lazily enjoying a cigarette and watching the slow grazing promenade of a pair of snow-geese, the male looking rather like an albino edition of the russet-hued female. Out of the corner of his eye Crosby also noted with some interest the hesitating hoverings of a human figure, which had passed and repassed his seat two or three times at shortening intervals, like a wary crow about to alight near some possibly edible morsel. Inevitably the figure came to an anchorage on the bench, within easy talking distance of its original occupant. The uncared-for clothes, the aggressive, grizzled beard, and the furtive, evasive eye of the new-comer bespoke the professional cadger, the man who would undergo hours of humiliating tale-spinning and rebuff rather than adventure on half a day's decent work.

For a while the new-comer fixed his eyes straight in front of him in a strenuous, unseeing gaze ; then his voice broke out with the insinuating inflection of one who has a story to retail well worth any loiterer's while to listen to.

"It's a strange world," he said.

As the statement met with no response he altered it to the form of a question.

"I dare say you've found it to be a strange world, mister?"

"As far as I am concerned," said Crosby, "the strangeness has worn off in the course of thirty-six years."

"Ah," said the greybeard, "I could tell you things that you'd hardly believe. Marvellous things that have really happened to me."

"Nowadays there is not demand for marvellous things that have really happened," said Crosby discouragingly; "the professional writers of fiction turn these things out so much better. For instance, my neighbours tell me wonderful, incredible things that their Aberdeens and chows and borzois have done; I never listen to them. On the other hand, I have read *The Hound of the Baskervilles* three times."

The greybeard moved uneasily in his seat; then he opened up new country.

"I take it that you are a professing Christian," he observed.

"I am a prominent and I think I may say an influential member of the Mussulman community of Eastern Persia," said Crosby, making an excursion himself into the realms of fiction.

The greybeard was obviously disconcerted at this new check of introductory conversation, but the defeat was only momentary.

"Persia. I should never have taken you for a Persian," he remarked, with a somewhat aggrieved air.

"I am not," said Crosby; "my father was an Afghan."

"An Afghan!" said the other, smitten into bewildered silence for a moment. Then he recovered himself and renewed his attack.

"Afghanistan. Ah! We've had some wars with that country; now, I dare say, instead of fighting it we might have learned something from it. A very wealthy country, I believe. No real poverty there."

He raised his voice on the word "poverty" with a suggestion of intense feeling. Crosby saw the opening and avoided it.

"It possesses, nevertheless, a number of highly talented and ingenious beggars," he said; "if I had not spoken so disparagingly of marvellous things that have really happened I would tell you the story of Ibrahim and the eleven camel-loads of blotting-paper. Also I have forgotten exactly how it ended."

"My own life-story is a curious one," said the stranger, apparently stifling all desire to hear the history of Ibrahim; "I was not always as you see me now."

"We are supposed to undergo complete change in the course of every seven years," said Crosby, as an explanation of the foregoing announcement.

"I mean I was not always in such distressing circumstances as I am at present," pursued the stranger doggedly.

"That sounds rather rude," said Crosby stiffly, "considering that you are at present talking to a man reputed to be one of the most gifted conversationalists of the Afghan border."

"I don't mean in that way," said the greybeard hastily; "I've been very much interested in your conversation. I was alluding to my unfortunate financial situation. You mayn't hardly believe it, but at the present moment I am absolutely without a farthing. Don't see any prospect of getting any money, either, for the next few days. I don't suppose you've ever found yourself in such a position," he added.

"In the town of Yom," said Crosby, "which is in Southern Afghanistan, and which also happens to be my birthplace, there was a Chinese philosopher who used to say that one of the three chiefest human blessings was to be absolutely without money. I forget what the other two were."

"Ah, I dare say," said the stranger, in a tone that betrayed no enthusiasm for the philosopher's memory; "and did he practise what he preached? That's the test."

"He lived happily with very little money or resources," said Crosby.

"Then I expect he had friends who would help him liberally whenever he was in difficulties, such as I am in at present."

"In Yom," said Crosby, "it is not necessary to have friends in order to obtain help. Any citizen of Yom would help a stranger as a matter of course."

The greybeard was now genuinely interested. The conversation had at last taken a favourable turn.

"If some one, like me, for instance, who was in undeserved difficulties, asked a citizen of that town you speak of for a small loan to tide over a few days' impecuniosity—five shillings, or perhaps a rather larger sum—would it be given to him as a matter of course?"

"There would be a certain preliminary," said Crosby; "one would take him to a wine-shop and treat him to a measure of wine, and then, after a little high-flown conversation, one would put the desired sum in his hand and wish him good-day. It is a roundabout way of performing a simple transaction, but in the East all ways are roundabout."

The listener's eyes were glittering.

"Ah," he exclaimed, with a thin sneer ringing meaningly through his words, "I suppose you've given up all those generous customs since you left your town. Don't practise them now, I expect."

"No one who has lived in Yom," said Crosby fervently, "and remembers its green hills covered with apricot and almond trees, and the cold water that rushes down like a caress from the upland snows and dashes under the little wooden bridges, no one who remembers these things and treasures the memory of them would ever give up a single one of its unwritten laws and customs. To me they are as binding as though I still lived in that hallowed home of my youth."

"Then if I was to ask you for a small loan——" began the greybeard fawningly, edging nearer on the seat and hurriedly wondering how large he might safely make his request, "if I was to ask you for, say——"

"At any other time, certainly," said Crosby; "in the months of November and December, however, it is absolutely forbidden for anyone of our race to give or receive loans or gifts; in fact, one does not willingly speak of them. It is considered unlucky. We will therefore close this discussion."

"But it is still October!" exclaimed the adventurer with an eager, angry whine, as Crosby rose from his seat; "wants eight days to the end of the month!"

"The Afghan November began yesterday," said

Crosby severely, and in another moment he was striding across the Park, leaving his recent companion scowling and muttering furiously on the seat.

"I don't believe a word of his story," he chattered to himself; "pack of nasty lies from beginning to end. Wish I'd told him so to his face. Calling himself an Afghan!"

The snorts and snarls that escaped from him for the next quarter of an hour went far to support the truth of the old saying that two of a trade never agree.

THE SCHARTZ-METTERKLUME METHOD

LADY CARLOTTA stepped out on to the platform of the small wayside station and took a turn or two up and down its uninteresting length, to kill time till the train should be pleased to proceed on its way. Then, in the roadway beyond, she saw a horse struggling with a more than ample load, and a carter of the sort that seems to bear a sullen hatred against the animal that helps him to earn a living. Lady Carlotta promptly betook her to the roadway, and put rather a different complexion on the struggle. Certain of her acquaintances were wont to give her plentiful admonition as to the undesirability of interfering on behalf of a distressed animal, such interference being " none of her business." Only once had she put the doctrine of non-interference into practice, when one of its most eloquent exponents had been besieged for nearly three hours in a small and extremely uncomfortable may-tree by an angry boar-pig, while Lady Carlotta, on the other side of the fence, had proceeded with the water-colour sketch she was engaged on, and refused to interfere between the boar and his prisoner. It is to be feared that she lost the friendship of the ultimately rescued lady. On this occasion she merely lost the train, which gave way to the first sign of impatience it had shown throughout the journey, and steamed off without her. She bore the desertion with philosophical indifference; her friends and relations were thoroughly well used to the fact of her luggage arriving without her. She wired a vague non-committal message to her destination to say that she was coming on "by another train." Before she had time to think what her next move might be she was confronted by an imposingly attired lady, who seemed to be taking a prolonged mental inventory of her clothes and looks.

"You must be Miss Hope, the governess I've come to meet," said the apparition, in a tone that admitted of very little argument.

"Very well, if I must I must," said Lady Carlotta to herself with dangerous meekness.

"I am Mrs. Quabarl," continued the lady; "and where, pray, is your luggage?"

"It's gone astray," said the alleged governess, falling in with the excellent rule of life that the absent are always to blame; the luggage had, in point of fact, behaved with perfect correctitude. "I've just telegraphed about it," she added, with a nearer approach to truth.

"How provoking," said Mrs. Quabarl; "these railway companies are so careless. However, my maid can lend you things for the night," and she led the way to her car.

During the drive to the Quabarl mansion Lady Carlotta was impressively introduced to the nature of the charge that had been thrust upon her; she learned that Claude and Wilfrid were delicate, sensitive young people, that Irene had the artistic temperament highly developed, and that Viola was something or other else of a mould equally commonplace among children of that class and type in the twentieth century.

"I wish them not only to be *taught*," said Mrs. Quabarl, "but *interested* in what they learn. In their history lessons, for instance, you must try to make them feel that they are being introduced to the life-stories of men and women who really lived, not merely committing a mass of names and dates to memory. French, of course, I shall expect you to talk at mealtimes several days in the week."

"I shall talk French four days of the week and Russian in the remaining three."

"Russian? My dear Miss Hope, no one in the house speaks or understands Russian."

"That will not embarrass me in the least," said Lady Carlotta coldly.

Mrs. Quabarl, to use a colloquial expression, was knocked off her perch. She was one of those imperfectly self-assured individuals who are magnificent and autocratic as long as they are not seriously opposed. The least show of unexpected resistance goes a long way towards rendering them cowed and apologetic. When the new governess failed to express wondering admiration of the large newly-purchased and expensive car, and lightly alluded to the superior advantages of one or two makes which had just been put on the market, the discomfiture of her patroness became almost abject. Her feelings were those which might have animated a general of ancient warfaring days, on beholding his heaviest battle-elephant ignominiously driven off the field by slingers and javelin throwers.

At dinner that evening, although reinforced by her husband, who usually duplicated her opinions and lent her moral support generally, Mrs. Quabarl regained none of her lost ground. The governess not only helped herself well and truly to wine, but held forth with considerable show of critical knowledge on various vintage matters, concerning which the Quabarls were in no wise able to pose as authorities. Previous governesses had limited their conversation on the wine topic to a respectful and doubtless sincere expression of a preference for water. When this one went as far as to recommend a wine firm in whose hands you could not go very far wrong Mrs. Quabarl thought it time to turn the conversation into more usual channels.

"We got very satisfactory references about you from Canon Teep," she observed; "a very estimable man, I should think."

"Drinks like a fish and beats his wife, otherwise a very lovable character," said the governess imperturbably.

"My *dear* Miss Hope! I trust you are exaggerating," exclaimed the Quabarls in unison.

"One must in justice admit that there is some provocation," continued the romancer. "Mrs. Teep is quite the most irritating bridge-player that I have ever sat down with; her leads and declarations would condone a certain amount of brutality in her partner, but to souse her with the contents of the only soda-water syphon in the house on a Sunday afternoon, when one couldn't get another, argues an indifference to the comfort of others which I cannot altogether overlook. You may think me hasty in my judgments, but it was practically on account of the syphon incident that I left."

"We will talk of this some other time," said Mrs. Quabarl hastily.

"I shall never allude to it again," said the governess with decision.

Mr. Quabarl made a welcome diversion by asking what studies the new instructress proposed to inaugurate on the morrow.

"History to begin with," she informed him.

"Ah, history," he observed sagely; "now in teaching them history you must take care to interest them in what they learn. You must make them feel that they are being introduced to the life-stories of men and women who really lived——"

"I've told her all that," interposed Mrs. Quabarl.

"I teach history on the Schartz-Metterklume method," said the governess loftily.

"Ah, yes," said her listeners, thinking it expedient to assume an acquaintance at least with the name.

"What are you children doing out here?" demanded Mrs. Quabarl the next morning, on finding Irene sitting rather glumly at the head of the stairs, while her sister was perched in an attitude of depressed discomfort on the window-seat behind her, with a wolf-skin rug almost covering her.

"We are having a history lesson," came the unexpected reply. "I am supposed to be Rome, and Viola up there is the she-wolf; not a real wolf, but the figure of one that the Romans used to set store by—I forget why. Claude and Wilfrid have gone to fetch the shabby women."

"The shabby women?"

"Yes, they've got to carry them off. They didn't want to, but Miss Hope got one of father's fives-bats and said she'd give them a number nine spanking if they didn't, so they've gone to do it."

A loud, angry screaming from the direction of the lawn drew Mrs. Quabarl thither in hot haste, fearful lest the threatened castigation might even now be in process of infliction. The outcry, however, came principally from the two small daughters of the lodge-keeper, who were being hauled and pushed towards the house by the panting and dishevelled Claude and Wilfrid, whose task was rendered even more arduous by the incessant, if not very effectual, attacks of the captured maidens' small brother. The governess, fives-bat in hand, sat negligently on the stone balustrade, presiding over the scene with the cold impartiality of a Goddess of Battles. A furious and repeated chorus of "I'll tell muvver" rose from the lodge children, but the lodge-mother, who was hard of hearing, was for the moment immersed in the preoccupation of her washtub. After an apprehensive glance in the direction of the lodge (the good woman was gifted with the highly militant temper which is sometimes the privilege of deafness) Mrs. Quabarl flew indignantly to the rescue of the struggling captives.

"Wilfrid! Claude! Let those children go at once. Miss Hope, what on earth is the meaning of this scene?"

"Early Roman history; the Sabine women, don't you know? It's the Schartz-Metterklume method to make children understand history by acting it themselves; fixes it in their memory, you know. Of course, if, thanks to your interference, your boys go through life thinking that the Sabine women ultimately escaped, I really cannot be held responsible."

"You may be very clever and modern, Miss Hope," said Mrs. Quabarl firmly, "but I should like you to leave here by the next train. Your luggage will be sent after you as soon as it arrives."

"I'm not certain exactly where I shall be for the next few days," said the dismissed instructress of youth; "you might keep my luggage till I wire my address. There are only a couple of trunks and some golf-clubs and a leopard cub."

"A leopard cub!" gasped Mrs. Quabarl. Even in her departure this extraordinary person seemed destined to leave a trail of embarrassment behind her.

"Well, it's rather left off being a cub; it's more than half-grown, you know. A fowl every day and a rabbit on Sundays is what it usually gets. Raw beef makes it too excitable. Don't trouble about getting the car for me, I'm rather inclined for a walk."

And Lady Carlotta strode out of the Quabarl horizon.

The advent of the genuine Miss Hope, who had made a mistake as to the day on which she was due to arrive, caused a turmoil which that good lady was quite unused to inspiring. Obviously the Quabarl family had been woefully befooled, but a certain amount of relief came with the knowledge.

"How tiresome for you, dear Carlotta," said her hostess, when the overdue guest ultimately arrived; "how very tiresome losing your train and having to stop overnight in a strange place."

"Oh dear, no," said Lady Carlotta; "not at all tiresome—for me."

THE SEVENTH PULLET

"IT'S not the daily grind that I complain of," said Blenkinthrope resentfully; "it's the dull grey sameness of my life outside of office hours. Nothing of interest comes my way, nothing remarkable or out of the common. Even the little things that I do try to find some interest in don't seem to interest other people. Things in my garden, for instance."

"The potato that weighed just over two pounds," said his friend Gorworth.

"Did I tell you about that?" said Blenkinthrope; "I was telling the others in the train this morning. I forgot if I'd told you."

"To be exact you told me that it weighed just under two pounds, but I took into account the fact that abnormal vegetables and freshwater fish have an after-life, in which growth is not arrested."

"You're just like the others," said Blenkinthrope sadly. "you only make fun of it."

"The fault is with the potato, not with us," said Gorworth; "we are not in the least interested in it because it is not in the least interesting. The men you go up in the train with every day are just in the same case as yourself; their lives are commonplace and not very interesting to themselves, and they certainly are not going to wax enthusiastic over the commonplace events in other men's lives. Tell them something startling, dramatic, piquant that has happened to yourself or to some one in your family, and you will capture their interest at once. They will talk about you with a certain personal pride to all their acquaintances. 'Man I know intimately, fellow called Blenkinthrope, lives down my way, had two of his fingers clawed clean off by a lobster he was carrying home to supper. Doctor says entire hand may have to come off.' Now that is conversation of a very high order. But imagine walking into a tennis club with the remark: 'I know a man who has grown a potato weighing two and a quarter pounds.'"

"But hang it all, my dear fellow," said Blenkinthrope impatiently, "haven't I just told you that nothing of a remarkable nature ever happens to me?"

"Invent something," said Gorworth. Since winning a prize for excellence in Scriptural knowledge at a preparatory school he had felt licensed to be a little more unscrupulous than the circle he moved in. Much might surely be excused to one who in early life could give a list of seventeen trees mentioned in the Old Testament.

"What sort of thing?" asked Blenkinthrope, somewhat snappishly.

"A snake got into your hen-run yesterday morning and killed six out of seven pullets, first mesmerizing them with its eyes and then biting them as they stood helpless. The seventh pullet was one of that French sort, with feathers all over its eyes, so it escaped the mesmeric snare, and just flew at what it could see of the snake and pecked it to pieces."

"Thank you," said Blenkinthrope stiffly; "it's a very clever invention. If such a thing had really happened in my poultry-run I admit I should have been proud and interested to tell people about it. But I'd rather stick to fact, even if it is plain fact." All the same his mind dwelt wistfully on the story of the Seventh Pullet. He could picture himself telling it in the train amid the absorbed interest of his fellow-passengers. Unconsciously all sorts of little details and improvements began to suggest themselves.

Wistfulness was still his dominant mood when he took his seat in the railway carriage the next morning. Opposite him sat Stevenham, who had attained to a recognized brevet of importance through the fact of an uncle having dropped dead in the act of voting at a Parliamentary election. That had happened three years ago, but Stevenham was still deferred to on all questions of home and foreign politics.

"Hullo, how's the giant mushroom, or whatever it was?" was all the notice Blenkinthrope got from his fellow travellers.

Young Duckby, whom he mildly disliked, speedily monopolized the general attention by an account of a domestic bereavement.

"Had four young pigeons carried off last night by a whacking big rat. Oh, a monster he must have been; you could tell by the size of the hole he made breaking into the loft."

No moderate-sized rat ever seemed to carry out any predatory operations in these regions; they were all enormous in their enormity.

"Pretty hard lines that," continued Duckby, seeing that he had secured the attention and respect of the company; "four squeakers carried off at one swoop. You'd find it rather hard to match that in the way of unlooked-for bad luck."

"I had six pullets out of a pen of seven killed by a snake yesterday afternoon," said Blenkinthrope, in a voice which he hardly recognized as his own.

"By a snake?" came in excited chorus.

"It fascinated them with its deadly, glittering

eyes, one after the other, and struck them down while they stood helpless. A bedridden neighbour, who wasn't able to call for assistance, witnessed it all from her bedroom window."

"Well, I never!" broke in the chorus, with variations.

"The interesting part of it is about the seventh pullet, the one that didn't get killed," resumed Blenkinthrope, slowly lighting a cigarette. His diffidence had left him, and he was beginning to realize how safe and easy depravity can seem once one has the courage to begin. "The six dead birds were Minorcas; the seventh was a Houdan with a mop of feathers all over its eyes. It could hardly see the snake at all, so of course it wasn't mesmerized like the others. It just could see something wriggling on the ground, and went for it and pecked it to death."

"Well, I'm blessed!" exclaimed the chorus.

In the course of the next few days Blenkinthrope discovered how little the loss of one's self-respect affects one when one has gained the esteem of the world. His story found its way into one of the poultry papers, and was copied thence into a daily news-sheet as a matter of general interest. A lady wrote from the North of Scotland recounting a similar episode which she had witnessed as occurring between a stoat and a blind grouse. Somehow a lie seems so much less reprehensible when one can call it a lee.

For awhile the adapter of the Seventh Pullet story enjoyed to the full his altered standing as a person of consequence, one who had had some share in the strange events of his times. Then he was thrust once again into the cold grey background by the sudden blossoming into importance of Smith-Paddon, a daily fellow-traveller, whose little girl had been knocked down and nearly hurt by a car belonging to a musical-comedy actress. The actress was not in the car at the time, but she was in numerous photographs which appeared in the illustrated papers of Zoto Dobreen inquiring after the well-being of Maisie, daughter of Edmund Smith-Paddon, Esq. With this new human interest to absorb them the travelling companions were almost rude when Blenkinthrope tried to explain his contrivance for keeping vipers and peregrine falcons out of his chicken-run.

Gorworth, to whom he unburdened himself in private, gave him the same counsel as theretofore.

"Invent something."

"Yes, but what?"

The ready affirmative coupled with the question betrayed a significant shifting of the ethical standpoint.

It was a few days later that Blenkinthrope revealed a chapter of family history to the customary gathering in the railway carriage.

"Curious thing happened to my aunt, the one who lives in Paris," he began. He had several aunts, but they were all geographically distributed over Greater London.

"She was sitting on a seat in the Bois the other afternoon, after lunching at the Roumanian Legation."

Whatever the story gained in picturesqueness for the dragging-in of diplomatic "atmosphere," it ceased from that moment to command any acceptance as a record of current events. Gorworth had warned his neophyte that this would be the case, but the traditional enthusiasm of the neophyte had triumphed over discretion.

"She was feeling rather drowsy, the effect probably of the champagne, which she's not in the habit of taking in the middle of the day."

A subdued murmur of admiration went round the company. Blenkinthrope's aunts were not used to taking champagne in the middle of the year, regarding it exclusively as a Christmas and New Year accessory.

"Presently a rather portly gentleman passed by her seat and paused an instant to light a cigar. At that moment a youngish man came up behind him, drew the blade from a swordstick, and stabbed him half a dozen times through and through. 'Scoundrel,' he cried to his victim, 'you do not know me. My name is Henri Leturc.' The elder man wiped away some of the blood that was spattering his clothes, turned to his assailant, and said: 'And since when has an attempted assassination been considered an introduction?' Then he finished lighting his cigar and walked away. My aunt had intended screaming for the police, but seeing the indifference with which the principal in the affair treated the matter she felt that it would be an impertinence on her part to interfere. Of course I need hardly say she put the whole thing down to the effects of a warm, drowsy afternoon and the Legation champagne. Now comes the astonishing part of my story. A fortnight later a bank manager was stabbed to death with a swordstick in that very part of the Bois. His assassin was the son of a charwoman formerly working at the bank, who had been dismissed from her job by the manager on account of chronic intemperance His name was Henri Leturc."

From that moment Blenkinthrope was tacitly accepted as the Munchausen of the party. No effort was spared to draw him out from day to day in the exercise of testing their powers of credulity, and Blenkinthrope, in the false security of an assured and receptive audience, waxed industrious and ingenious in supplying the demand for marvels. Duckby's satirical story of a tame otter that had a tank in the garden to swim in, and whined restlessly whenever the water-rate was overdue, was scarcely an unfair parody of some of Blenkinthrope's wilder efforts. And then one day came Nemesis.

Returning to his villa one evening Blenkinthrope found his wife sitting in front of a pack of cards, which she was scrutinizing with unusual concentration.

"The same old patience-game?" he asked carelessly.

"No, dear; this is the Death's Head patience, the most difficult of them all. I've never got it to work out, and somehow I should be rather frightened if I did. Mother only got it out once in her life; she was afraid of it, too. Her great-aunt had done it once and fallen dead from excitement the next moment, and mother always had a feeling that she would die if she ever got it out. She died the same night that she did it. She was in bad health at the time, certainly, but it was a strange coincidence."

"Don't do it if it frightens you," was Blenkinthrope's practical comment as he left the room. A few minutes later his wife called to him.

"John, it gave me such a turn, I nearly got it out. Only the five of diamonds held me up at the end. I really thought I'd done it."

"Why, you can do it," said Blenkinthrope, who had come back to the room; "if you shift the eight of clubs on to that open nine the five can be moved on to the six."

His wife made the suggested move with hasty, trembling fingers, and piled the outstanding cards on to their respective packs. Then she followed the example of her mother and great-grand-aunt.

Blenkinthrope had been genuinely fond of his wife, but in the midst of his bereavement one dominant thought obtruded itself. Something sensational and real had at last come into his life; no longer was it a grey, colourless record. The head-lines which might appropriately describe his domestic tragedy kept shaping themselves in his brain. "Inherited presentiment comes true." "The Death's Head patience: Card-game that justified its sinister name in three generations." He wrote out a full story of the fatal occurrence for the *Essex Vedette*, the editor of which was a friend of his, and to another friend he gave a condensed account, to be taken up to the office of one of the halfpenny dailies. But in both cases his reputation as a romancer stood fatally in the way of the fulfilment of his ambitions. "Not the right thing to be Munchausening in a time of sorrow" agreed his friends among themselves, and a brief note of regret at the "sudden death of the wife of our respected neighbour, Mr. John Blenkinthrope, from heart failure," appearing in the news column of the local paper was the forlorn outcome of his visions of widespread publicity.

Blenkinthrope shrank from the society of his erstwhile travelling companions and took to travelling townwards by an earlier train. He sometimes tries to enlist the sympathy and attention of a chance acquaintance in details of the whistling prowess of his best canary or the dimensions of his largest beet-root; he scarcely recognizes himself as the man who was once spoken about and pointed out as the owner of the Seventh Pullet.

THE BLIND SPOT

"YOU'VE just come back from Adelaide's funeral, haven't you?" said Sir Lulworth to his nephew; "I suppose it was very like most other funerals?"

"I'll tell you all about it at lunch," said Egbert.

"You'll do nothing of the sort. It wouldn't be respectful either to your great-aunt's memory or to the lunch. We begin with Spanish olives, then a borshch, then more olives and a bird of some kind, and a rather enticing Rhenish wine, not at all expensive as wines go in this country, but still quite laudable in its way. Now there's absolutely nothing in that menu that harmonizes in the least with the subject of your great-aunt Adelaide or her funeral. She was a charming woman, and quite as intelligent as she had any need to be, but somehow she always reminded me of an English cook's idea of a Madras curry."

"She used to say you were frivolous," said Egbert. Something in his tone suggested that he rather endorsed the verdict.

"I believe I once considerably scandalized her by declaring that clear soup was a more important factor in life than a clear conscience. She had very little sense of proportion. By the way, she made you her principal heir, didn't she?"

"Yes," said Egbert, "and executor as well. It's in that connection that I particularly want to speak to you."

"Business is not my strong point at any time," said Sir Lulworth, "and certainly not when we're on the immediate threshold of lunch."

"It isn't exactly business," explained Egbert, as he followed his uncle into the dining-room. "It's something rather serious. Very serious."

"Then we can't possibly speak about it now," said Sir Lulworth; "no one could talk seriously, during a borshch. A beautifully constructed borshch, such as you are going to experience presently, ought not only to banish conversation but almost to annihilate thought. Later on, when we arrive at the second stage of olives, I shall be quite ready to discuss that new book on Borrow, or, if you prefer it, the present situation in the Grand Duchy of Luxemburg. But I absolutely decline to talk anything approaching business till we have finished with the bird."

For the greater part of the meal Egbert sat in an abstracted silence, the silence of a man whose mind is focussed on one topic. When the coffee stage had been reached he launched himself suddenly athwart his uncle's reminiscences of the Court of Luxemburg.

"I think I told you that great-aunt Adelaide had made me her executor. There wasn't very much to be done in the way of legal matters, but I had to go through her papers."

"That would be a fairly heavy task in itself. I should imagine there were reams of family letters."

"Stacks of them, and most of them highly uninteresting. There was one packet, however, which I thought might repay a careful perusal. It was a bundle of correspondence from her brother Peter."

"The Canon of tragic memory," said Lulworth.

"Exactly, of tragic memory, as you say; a tragedy that has never been fathomed."

"Probably the simplest explanation was the correct one," said Sir Lulworth; "he slipped on the stone staircase and fractured his skull in falling."

Egbert shook his head. "The medical evidence all went to prove that the blow on the head was struck by some one coming up behind him. A wound caused by violent contact with the steps could not possibly have been inflicted at that angle of the skull. They experimented with a dummy figure falling in every conceivable position."

"But the motive?" exclaimed Sir Lulworth; "no one had any interest in doing away with him, and the number of people who destroy Canons of the Established Church for the mere fun of killing must be extremely limited. Of course there are individuals of weak mental balance who do that sort of thing, but they seldom conceal their handiwork; they are more generally inclined to parade it."

"His cook was under suspicion," said Egbert shortly.

"I know he was," said Sir Lulworth, "simply because he was about the only person on the premises at the time of the tragedy. But could anything be sillier than trying to fasten a charge of murder on to Sebastien? He had nothing to gain, in fact, a good deal to lose, from the death of his employer. The Canon was paying him quite as good wages as I was able to offer him when I took him over into my service. I have since raised them to something a little more in accordance with his real worth, but at the time he was glad to find a new place without troubling about an increase of wages. People were fighting rather shy of him, and he had no friends in this country. No; if anyone in the world was interested in the prolonged life and unimpaired digestion of the Canon it would certainly be Sebastien."

"People don't always weigh the consequences of their rash acts," said Egbert, "otherwise there would be very few murders committed. Sebastien is a man of hot temper."

"He is a southerner," admitted Sir Lulworth; "to be geographically exact I believe he hails from the French slopes of the Pyrenees. I took that into consideration when he nearly killed the gardener's boy the other day for bringing him a spurious substitute for sorrel. One must always make allowances for origin and locality and early environment; 'Tell me your longitude and I'll know what latitude to allow you,' is my motto."

"There, you see," said Egbert, "he nearly killed the gardener's boy."

"My dear Egbert, between nearly killing a gardener's boy and altogether killing a Canon there is a wide difference. No doubt you have often felt a temporary desire to kill a gardener's boy; you have never given way to it, and I respect you for your self-control. But I don't suppose you have ever wanted to kill an octogenarian Canon. Besides, as far as we know, there had never been any quarrel or disagreement between the two men. The evidence at the inquest brought that out very clearly."

"Ah!" said Egbert, with the air of a man coming at last into a deferred inheritance of conversational importance, "that is precisely what I want to speak to you about."

He pushed away his coffee cup and drew a pocket-book from his inner breast-pocket. From the depths of the pocket-book he produced an envelope, and from the envelope he extracted a letter, closely written in a small, neat handwriting.

"One of the Canon's numerous letters to Aunt Adelaide," he explained, "written a few days before his death. Her memory was already failing when she received it, and I dare say she forgot the contents as soon as she had read it; otherwise, in the light of what subsequently happened, we should have heard something of this letter before now. If it had been produced at the inquest I fancy it would have made some difference in the course of affairs. The evidence, as you remarked just now, choked off suspicion against Sebastien by disclosing an utter absence of anything that could be considered a motive or provocation for the crime, if crime there was."

"Oh, read the letter," said Sir Lulworth impatiently.

"It's a long rambling affair, like most of his letters in his later years," said Egbert. "I'll read the part that bears immediately on the mystery.

"'I very much fear I shall have to get rid of Sebastien. He cooks divinely, but he has the temper of a fiend or an anthropoid ape, and I am really in bodily fear of him. We had a dispute the other day as to the correct sort of lunch to be served on Ash Wednesday, and I got so irritated and annoyed at his conceit and obstinacy that at last I threw a cupful of coffee in his face and called him at the same time an impudent jackanapes. Very little of the coffee went actually in his face, but I have never seen a human being show such deplorable lack of self-control. I laughed at the threat of killing me that he spluttered out in his rage, and thought the whole thing would blow over, but I have several times since caught him scowling and muttering in a highly unpleasant fashion, and lately I have fancied that he was dogging my footsteps about the grounds, particularly when I walk of an evening in the Italian Garden.'

" It was on the steps in the Italian Garden that the body was found," commented Egbert, and resumed reading.

" 'I dare say the danger is imaginary; but I shall feel more at ease when he has quitted my service.' "

Egbert paused for a moment at the conclusion of the extract; then, as his uncle made no remark, he added: " If lack of motive was the only factor that saved Sebastien from prosecution I fancy this letter will put a different complexion on matters."

" Have you shown it to anyone else?" asked Sir Lulworth, reaching out his hand for the incriminating piece of paper.

" No," said Egbert, handing it across the table, " I thought I would tell you about it first. Heavens, what are you doing?"

Egbert's voice rose almost to a scream. Sir Lulworth had flung the paper well and truly into the glowing centre of the grate. The small, neat handwriting shrivelled into black flaky nothingness.

" What on earth did you do that for?" gasped Egbert. " That letter was our one piece of evidence to connect Sebastien with the crime."

" That is why I destroyed it," said Sir Lulworth.

" But why should you want to shield him?" cried Egbert; " the man is a common murderer."

" A common murderer, possibly, but a very uncommon cook."

DUSK

NORMAN GORTSBY sat on a bench in the Park, with his back to a strip of bush-planted sward, fenced by the park railings, and the Row fronting him across a wide stretch of carriage drive. Hyde Park Corner, with its rattle and hoot of traffic, lay immediately to his right. It was some thirty minutes past six on an early March evening, and dusk had fallen heavily over the scene, dusk mitigated by some faint moonlight and many street lamps. There was a wide emptiness over road and side walk, and yet there were many unconsidered figures moving silently through the half-light or dotted unobtrusively on bench and chair, scarcely to be distinguished from the shadowed gloom in which they sat.

The scene pleased Gortsby and harmonized with his present mood. Dusk, to his mind, was the hour of the defeated. Men and women, who had fought and lost, who hid their fallen fortunes and dead hopes as far as possible from the scrutiny of the curious, came forth in this hour of gloaming, when their shabby clothes and bowed shoulders and unhappy eyes might pass unnoticed, or, at any rate, unrecognized.

> A king that is conquered must see strange looks,
> So bitter a thing is the heart of man.

The wanderers in the dusk did not choose to have strange looks fasten on them, therefore they came out in this bat-fashion, taking their pleasure sadly in a pleasure-ground that had emptied of its rightful occupants. Beyond the sheltering screen of bushes and palings came a realm of brilliant lights and noisy, rushing traffic. A blazing, many-tiered stretch of windows shone through the dusk and almost dispersed it, marking the haunts of those other people, who held their own in life's struggle, or at any rate had not had to admit failure. So Gortsby's imagination pictured things as he sat on his bench in the almost deserted walk. He was in the mood to count himself among the defeated. Money troubles did not press on him ; had he so wished he could have strolled into the thoroughfares of light and noise, and taken his place among the jostling ranks of those who enjoyed prosperity or struggled for it. He had failed in a more subtle ambition, and for the moment he was heart sore and disillusionized, and not disinclined to take a certain cynical pleasure in observing and labelling his fellow wanderers as they went their ways in the dark stretches between the lamp-lights.

On the bench by his side sat an elderly gentleman with a drooping air of defiance that was probably the remaining vestige of self-respect in an individual who had ceased to defy successfully anybody or anything. His clothes could scarcely be called shabby, at least they passed muster in the half-light, but one's imagination could not have pictured the wearer embarking on the purchase of a half-crown box of chocolates or laying out ninepence on a carnation buttonhole. He belonged unmistakably to that forlorn orchestra to whose piping no one dances ; he was one of the world's lamenters who induces no responsive weeping. As he rose to go Gortsby imagined him returning to a home circle where he was snubbed and of no account, or to some bleak lodging where his ability to pay a weekly bill was the beginning and end of the interest he inspired. His retreating figure vanished slowly into the shadows, and his place on the bench was taken almost immediately by a young man, fairly well dressed but scarcely more cheerful of mien than his predecessor. As if to emphasize the fact that the world went badly with him the new-comer unburdened himself of an angry and very audible expletive as he flung himself into the seat.

"You don't seem in a very good temper," said Gortsby, judging that he was expected to take due notive of the demonstration.

The young man turned to him with a look of disarming frankness which put him instantly on his guard.

"You wouldn't be in a good temper if you were in the fix I'm in," he said; "I've done the silliest thing I've ever done in my life."

"Yes?" said Gortsby dispassionately.

"Came up this afternoon, meaning to stay at the Patagonian Hotel in Berkshire Square,' continued the young man; "when I got there I found it had been pulled down some weeks ago and a cinema theatre run up on the site. The taxi driver recommended me to another hotel some way off and I went there. I just sent a letter to my people, giving them the address, and then I went out to buy some soap—I'd forgotten to pack any and I hate using hotel soap. Then I strolled about a bit, had a drink at a bar and looked at the shops, and when I came to turn my steps back to the hotel I suddenly realized that I didn't remember its name or even what street it was in. There's a nice predicament for a fellow who hasn't any friends or connections in London! Of course I can wire to my people for the address, but they won't have got my letter till to morrow; meantime I'm without any money, came out with about a shilling on me, which went in buying the soap and getting the drink, and here I am, wandering about with twopence in my pocket and nowhere to go for the night."

There was an eloquent pause after the story had been told. "I suppose you think I've spun you rather an impossible yarn," said the young man presently, with a suggestion of resentment in his voice.

"Not at all impossible," said Gortsby judicially; "I remember doing exactly the same thing once in a foreign capital, and on that occasion there were two of us, which made it more remarkable. Luckily we remembered that the hotel was on a sort of canal, and when we struck the canal we were able to find our way back to the hotel."

The youth brightened at the reminiscence. "In a foreign city I wouldn't mind so much," he said; "one could go to one's Consul and get the requisite help from him. Here in one's own land one is far more derelict if one gets into a fix. Unless I can find some decent chap to swallow my story and lend me some money I seem likely to spend the night on the Embankment. I'm glad, anyhow, that you don't think the story outrageously improbable."

He threw a good deal of warmth into the last remark, as though perhaps to indicate his hope that Gortsby did not fall far short of the requisite decency.

"Of course," said Gortsby slowly, "the weak point of your story is that you can't produce the soap."

The young man sat forward hurriedly, felt rapidly in the pockets of his overcoat, and then jumped to his feet.

"I must have lost it," he muttered angrily.

"To lose an hotel and a cake of soap on one afternoon suggests wilful carelessness," said Gortsby, but the young man scarcely waited to hear the end of the remark. He flitted away down the path, his head held high, with an air of somewhat jaded jauntiness.

"It was a pity," mused Gortsby; "the going out to get one's own soap was the one convincing touch in the whole story, and yet it was just that little detail that brought him to grief. If he had had the brilliant forethought to provide himself with a cake of soap, wrapped and sealed with all the solicitude of the chemist's counter, he would have been a genius in his particular line. In his particular line genius certainly consists of an infinite capacity for taking precautions."

With that reflection Gortsby rose to go; as he did so an exclamation of concern escaped him. Lying on the ground by the side of the bench was a small oval packet, wrapped and sealed with the solicitude of a chemist's counter. It could be nothing else but a cake of soap, and it had evidently fallen out of the youth's overcoat pocket when he flung himself down on the seat. In another moment Gortsby was scudding along the dusk-shrouded path in anxious quest for a youthful figure in a light overcoat. He had nearly given up the search when he caught sight of the object of his pursuit standing irresolutely on the border of the carriage drive, evidently uncertain whether to strike across the Park or make for the bustling pavements of Knightsbridge. He turned round sharply with an air of defensive hostility when he found Gortsby hailing him.

"The important witness to the genuineness of your story has turned up," said Gortsby, holding out the cake of soap; "it must have slid out of your overcoat pocket when you sat down on the seat. I saw it on the ground after you left. You must excuse my disbelief, but appearances were really rather against you, and now, as I appealed to the testimony of the soap I think I ought to abide by its verdict. If the loan of a sovereign is any good to you——"

The young man hastily removed all doubt on the subject by pocketing the coin.

"Here is my card with my address," continued Gortsby; "any day this week will do for returning the money, and here is the soap—don't lose it again; it's been a good friend to you."

"Lucky thing your finding it," said the youth, and then, with a catch in his voice, he blurted out a word or two of thanks and fled headlong in the direction of Knightsbridge.

"Poor boy, he as nearly as possible broke down," said Gortsby to himself. "I don't wonder either; the relief from his quandary must have been acute. It's a lesson to me not to be too clever in judging by circumstances."

As Gortsby retraced his steps past the seat where the little drama had taken place he saw an elderly gentleman poking and peering beneath it and on all sides of it, and recognized his earlier fellow occupant.

"Have you lost anything, sir?" he asked.

"Yes, sir, a cake of soap."

A TOUCH OF REALISM

"I HOPE you've come full of suggestions for Christmas," said Lady Blonze to her latest arrived guest; "the old-fashioned Christmas and the up-to-date Christmas are both so played out. I want to have something really original this year."

"I was staying with the Mathesons last month," said Blanche Boveal eagerly, "and we had such a good idea. Every one in the house-party had to be a character and behave consistently all the time, and at the end of the visit one had to guess what every one's character was. The one who was voted to have acted his or her character best got a prize."

"It sounds amusing," said Lady Blonze.

"I was St. Francis of Assisi," continued Blanche; "we hadn't got to keep to our right sexes. I kept getting up in the middle of a meal and throwing out food to the birds; you see, the chief thing that one remembers of St. Francis is that he was fond of the birds. Every one was so stupid about it, and thought that I was the old man who feeds the sparrows in the Tuileries Gardens. Then Colonel Pentley was the Jolly Miller on the banks of Dee."

"How on earth did he do that?" asked Bertie van Tahn.

"'He laughed and sang from morn till night,'" explained Blanche.

"How dreadful for the rest of you," said Bertie;

"and anyway he wasn't on the banks of Dee."

"One had to imagine that," said Blanche.

"If you could imagine all that you might as well imagine cattle on the further bank and keep on calling them home, Mary-fashion, across the sands of Dee. Or you might change the river to the Yarrow and imagine it was on the top of you, and say you were Willie, or whoever it was, drowned in Yarrow."

"Of course it's easy to make fun of it," said Blanche sharply, "but it was extremely interesting and amusing. The prize was rather a fiasco, though. You see, Millie Matheson said her character was Lady Bountiful, and as she was our hostess, of course we all had to vote that she carried out her character better than anyone. Otherwise I ought to have got the prize."

"It's quite an idea for a Christmas party," said Lady Blonze; "we must certainly do it here."

Sir Nicholas was not so enthusiastic. "Are you quite sure, my dear, that you're wise in doing this thing?" he said to his wife when they were alone together. "It might do very well at the Mathesons, where they had rather a staid, elderly house-party, but here it will be a different matter. There is the Durmot flapper, for instance, who simply stops at nothing, and you know what Van Tahn is like. Then there is Cyril Skatterly; he has madness on one side of his family and a Hungarian grandmother on the other."

"I don't see what they could do that would matter," said Lady Blonze.

"It's the unknown that is to be dreaded," said Sir Nicholas. "If Skatterly took it into his head to represent a Bull of Bashan, well, I'd rather not be here."

"Of course we shan't allow any Bible characters.

Besides, I don't know what the Bulls of Bashan really did that was so very dreadful ; they just came round and gaped, as far as I remember."

"My dear, you don't know what Skatterly's Hungarian imagination mightn't read into the part ; it would be small satisfaction to say to him afterwards : 'You've behaved as no Bull of Bashan would have behaved.'"

"Oh, you're an alarmist," said Lady Blonze ; "I particularly want to have this idea carried out. It will be sure to be talked about a lot."

"That is quite possible," said Sir Nicholas.

. . . . .

Dinner that evening was not a particularly lively affair ; the strain of trying to impersonate a self-imposed character or to glean hints of identity from other people's conduct acted as a check on the natural festivity of such a gathering. There was a general feeling of gratitude and acquiescence when good-natured Rachel Klammerstein suggested that there should be an hour or two's respite from "the game" while they all listened to a little piano-playing after dinner. Rachel's love of piano music was not indiscriminate, and concentrated itself chiefly on selections rendered by her idolized offspring, Moritz and Augusta, who, to do them justice, played remarkably well.

The Klammersteins were deservedly popular as Christmas guests ; they gave expensive gifts lavishly on Christmas Day and New Year, and Mrs. Klammerstein had already dropped hints of her intention to present the prize for the best enacted character in the game competition. Every one had brightened at this prospect ; if it had fallen to Lady Blonze, as hostess, to provide the prize, she would have considered that a little souvenir of some twenty or twenty-five shillings' value would meet the case, whereas coming from a Klammerstein source it would certainly run to several guineas.

The close time for impersonation efforts came to an end with the final withdrawal of Moritz and Augusta from the piano. Blanche Boveal retired early, leaving the room in a series of laboured leaps that she hoped might be recognized as a tolerable imitation of Pavlova. Vera Durmot, the sixteen-year-old flapper, expressed her confident opinion that the performance was intended to typify Mark Twain's famous jumping frog, and her diagnosis of the case found general acceptance. Another guest to set an example of early bed-going was Waldo Plubley, who conducted his life on a minutely regulated system of time-tables and hygienic routine. Waldo was a plump, indolent young man of seven-and-twenty, whose mother had early in his life decided for him that he was unusually delicate, and by dint of much coddling and home-keeping had succeeded in making him physically soft and mentally peevish. Nine hours' unbroken sleep, preceded by elaborate breathing exercises and other hygienic ritual, was among the indispensable regulations which Waldo imposed on himself, and there were innumerable small observances which he exacted from those who were in any way obliged to minister to his requirements ; a special teapot for the decoction of his early tea was always solemnly handed over to the bedroom staff of any house in which he happened to be staying. No one had ever quite mastered the mechanism of this precious vessel, but Bertie van Tahn was responsible for the legend that its spout had to be kept facing north during the process of infusion.

On this particular night the irreducible nine hou[rs] were severely mutilated by the sudden and by no mea[ns] noiseless incursion of a pyjama-clad figure into Waldo['s] room at an hour midway between midnight an[d] dawn.

"What is the matter? What are you lookin[g] for?" asked the awakened and astonished Waldo[,] slowly recognizing Van Tahn, who appeared to b[e] searching hastily for somethng he had lost.

"Looking for sheep," was the reply.

"Sheep?" exclaimed Waldo.

"Yes, sheep. You don't suppose I'm looking fo[r] giraffes, do you?"

"I don't see why you should expect to find either in my room," retorted Waldo furiously.

"I can't argue the matter at this hour of the night," said Bertie, and began hastily rummaging in the chest of drawers. Shirts and underwear went flying on to the floor.

"There are no sheep here, I tell you," screamed Waldo.

"I've only got your word for it," said Bertie, whisking most of the bedclothes on to the floor; "if you weren't concealing something you wouldn't be so agitated."

Waldo was by this time convinced that Van Tahn was raving mad, and made an anxious effort to humour him.

"Go back to bed like a dear fellow," he pleaded, "and your sheep will turn up all right in the morning."

"I dare say," said Bertie gloomily, "without their tails. Nice fool I shall look with a lot of Manx sheep."

And by way of emphasizing his annoyance at the

rospect he sent Waldo's pillows flying to the top of
ıe wardrobe.

"But *why* no tails?" asked Waldo, whose teeth
vere chattering with fear and rage and lowered
emperature.

"My dear boy, have you never heard the ballad
f Little Bo-Peep?" said Bertie with a chuckle.
'It's my character in the Game, you know. If I
idn't go hunting about for my lost sheep no one would
e able to guess who I was; and now go to sleepy
weeps like a good child or I shall be cross with
ou."

"I leave you to imagine," wrote Waldo in the
ourse of a long letter to his mother, "how much
leep I was able to recover that night, and you know
how essential nine uninterrupted hours of slumber
are to my health."

On the other hand he was able to devote some
wakeful hours to exercises in breathing wrath and fury
against Bertie van Tahn.

Breakfast at Blonzecourt was a scattered meal, on
the "come when you please" principle, but the house-
party was supposed to gather in full strength at lunch.
On the day after the "Game" had been started there
were, however, some notable absentees. Waldo
Plubley, for instance, was reported to be nursing a headache. A large breakfast and an "A.B.C." had been
taken up to his room, but he had made no appearance
in the flesh.

"I expect he's playing up to some character," said
Vera Durmot; "isn't there a thing of Molière's,
'*Le Malade Imaginaire*'? I expect he's that."

Eight or nine lists came out, and were duly pencilled
with the suggestion.

"And where are the Klammersteins?" asked Lady Blonze; "they're usually so punctual."

"Another character pose, perhaps," said Bertie van Tahn; "'the Lost Ten Tribes.'"

"But there are only three of them. Besides, they'll want their lunch. Hasn't anyone seen anything of them?"

"Didn't you take them out in your car?" asked Blanche Boveal, addressing herself to Cyril Skatterly.

"Yes, took them out to Slogberry Moor immediately after breakfast. Miss Durmot came too."

"I saw you and Vera come back," said Lady Blonze, "but I didn't see the Klammersteins. Did you put them down in the village?"

"No," said Skatterly shortly.

"But where are they? Where did you leave them?"

"We left them on Slogberry Moor," said Vera calmly.

"On Slogberry Moor? Why, it's more than thirty miles away! How are they going to get back?"

"We didn't stop to consider that," said Skatterly; "we asked them to get out for a moment, on the pretence that the car had stuck, and then we dashed off full speed and left them there."

"But how dare you do such a thing? It's most inhuman! Why, it's been snowing for the last hour."

"I expect there'll be a cottage or farmhouse somewhere if they walk a mile or two."

"But why on earth have you done it?"

The question came in a chorus of indignant bewilderment.

"*That* would be telling what our characters are meant to be," said Vera.

"Didn't I warn you?" said Sir Nicholas tragically to his wife.

"It's something to do with Spanish history; we don't mind giving you that clue," said Skatterly, helping himself cheerfully to salad, and then Bertie van Tahn broke forth into peals of joyous laughter.

"I've got it! Ferdinand and Isabella deporting the Jews! Oh, lovely! Those two have certainly won the prize; we shan't get anything to beat that for thoroughness."

Lady Blonze's Christmas party was talked about and written about to an extent that she had not anticipated in her most ambitious moments. The letters from Waldo's mother would alone have made it memorable.

COUSIN TERESA

BASSET HARROWCLUFF returned to the home of his fathers, after an absence of four years, distinctly well pleased with himself. He was only thirty-one, but he had put in some useful service in an out-of-the-way, though not unimportant, corner of the world. He had quieted a province, kept open a trade route, enforced the tradition of respect which is worth the ransom of many kings in out-of-the-way regions, and done the whole business on rather less expenditure than would be requisite for organizing a charity in the home country. In Whitehall and places where they think, they doubtless thought well of him. It was not inconceivable, his father allowed himself to imagine, that Basset's name might figure in the next list of Honours.

Basset was inclined to be rather contemptuous of his half-brother, Lucas, whom he found feverishly engrossed in the same medley of elaborate futilities that had claimed his whole time and energies, such as they were, four years ago, and almost as far back before that as he could remember. It was the contempt of the man of action for the man of activities, and it was probably reciprocated. Lucas was an over-well nourished individual, some nine years Basset's senior, with a colouring that would have been accepted as a sign of intensive culture in an asparagus, but probably meant in this case mere abstention from exercise. His hair and forehead furnished a recessional note in a personality that was in all other respects obtrusive and assertive. There was certainly no Semitic blood in Lucas's parentage, but his appearance contrived to convey at least a suggestion of Jewish extraction. Clovis Sangrail, who knew most of his associates by sight, said it was undoubtedly a case of protective mimicry.

Two days after Basset's return, Lucas frisked in to lunch in a state of twittering excitement that could not be restrained even for the immediate consideration of soup, but had to be verbally discharged in spluttering competition with mouthfuls of vermicelli.

"I've got hold of an idea for something immense," he babbled, "something that is simply It."

Basset gave a short laugh that would have done equally well as a snort, if one had wanted to make the exchange. His half-brother was in the habit of discovering futilities that were "simply It" at frequently recurring intervals. The discovery generally meant that he flew up to town, preceded by glowingly-worded telegrams, to see some one connected with the stage or the publishing world, got together one or two momentous luncheon parties, flitted in and out of "Gambrinus" for one or two evenings, and returned home with an air of subdued importance and the asparagus tint slightly intensified. The great idea was generally forgotten a few weeks later in the excitement of some new discovery.

"The inspiration came to me whilst I was dressing," announced Lucas; "it will be *the* thing in the next music-hall *revue*. All London will go mad over it. It's just a couplet; of course there will be other words, but they won't matter. Listen:

Cousin Teresa takes out Cæsar,
Fido, Jock, and the big borzoi.

A lilting, catchy sort of refrain, you see, and big-drum business on the two syllables of bor-zoi. It's immense. And I've thought out all the business of it; the singer will sing the first verse alone, then during the second verse Cousin Teresa will walk through, followed by four wooden dogs on wheels; Cæsar will be an Irish terrier, Fido a black poodle, Jock a fox-terrier, and the borzoi, of course, will be a borzoi. During the third verse Cousin Teresa will come on alone, and the dogs will be drawn across by themselves from the opposite wing; then Cousin Teresa will catch on to the singer and go off-stage in one direction, while dogs' procession goes off in the other, crossing *en route*, which is always very effective. There'll be a lot of applause there, and for the fourth verse Cousin Teresa will come on in sables and the dogs will all have coats on. Then I've got a great idea for the fifth verse; each of the dogs will be led on by a Nut, and Cousin Teresa will come on from the opposite side, crossing *en route*, always effective, and then she turns round and leads the whole lot of them off on a string, and all the time every one singing like mad:

Cousin Teresa takes out Cæsar,
Fido, Jock, and the big borzoi.

Tum-Tum! Drum business on the two last syllables. I'm so excited, I shan't sleep a wink to-night. I'm off to-morrow by the ten-fifteen. I've wired to Hermanova to lunch with me."

If any of the rest of the family felt any excitement over the creation of Cousin Teresa, they were signally successful in concealing the fact.

"Poor Lucas does take his silly little ideas seriously," said Colonel Harrowcluff afterwards in the smoking-room.

"Yes," said his younger son, in a slightly less tolerant tone, "in a day or two he'll come back and tell us that his sensational masterpiece is above the heads of the public, and in about three weeks' time he'll be wild with enthusiasm over a scheme to dramatize the poems of Herrick or something equally promising."

And then an extraordinary thing befell. In defiance of all precedent Lucas's glowing anticipations were justified and endorsed by the course of events. If Cousin Teresa was above the heads of the public, the public heroically adapted itself to her altitude. Introduced as an experiment at a dull moment in a new *revue*, the success of the item was unmistakable; the calls were so insistent and uproarious that even Lucas's ample devisings of additional "business" scarcely sufficed to keep pace with the demand. Packed houses on successive evenings confirmed the verdict of the first night audience, stalls and boxes filled significantly just before the turn came on, and emptied significantly after the last *encore* had been given. The manager tearfully acknowledged that Cousin Teresa was It. Stage hands and supers and programme sellers acknowledged it to one another without the least reservation. The name of the *revue* dwindled to secondary importance, and vast letters of electric blue blazoned the words "Cousin Teresa" from the front of the great palace of pleasure. And of course, the magic of the famous refrain laid its spell all over the Metropolis. Restaurant proprietors were obliged to provide the members of their orchestras with painted wooden dogs on wheels, in order that the much-demanded and always conceded melody should be rendered with the necessary spectacular effects, and the crash of bottles and forks on the tables at the mention of the big borzoi usually drowned the sincerest efforts of drum or cymbals. Nowhere and at no time could one get away from the double thump that brought up the rear of the refrain; revellers reeling home at night banged it on doors and hoardings, milkmen clashed their cans to its cadence, messenger boys hit smaller messenger boys resounding double smacks on the same principle. And the more thoughtful circles of the great city were not deaf to the claims and significance of the popular melody. An enterprising and emancipated preacher discoursed from his pulpit on the inner meaning of "Cousin Teresa," and Lucas Harrowcluff was invited to lecture on the subject of his great achievement to members of the Young Men's Endeavour League, the Nine Arts Club, and other learned and willing-to-learn bodies. In Society it seemed to be the one thing people really cared to talk about; men and women of middle age and average education might be seen together in corners earnestly discussing, not the question whether Servia should have an outlet on the Adriatic, or the possibilities of a British success in international polo contests, but the more absorbing topic of the problematic Aztec or Nilotic origin of the Teresa *motiv*.

"Politics and patriotism are so boring and so out of date," said a revered lady who had some pretensions to oracular utterance; "we are too cosmopolitan nowadays to be really moved by them. That is why one welcomes an intelligible production like 'Cousin

Teresa,' that has a genuine message for one. One can't understand the message all at once, of course, but one felt from the very first that it was there. I've been to see it eighteen times and I'm going again to-morrow and on Thursday. One can't see it often enough."

. . . . .

"It would be rather a popular move if we gave this Harrowcluff person a knighthood or something of the sort," said the Minister reflectively.

"Which Harrowcluff?" asked his secretary.

"Which? There is only one, isn't there?" said the Minister; "the 'Cousin Teresa' man, of course. I think every one would be pleased if we knighted him. Yes, you can put him down on the list of certainties—under the letter L."

"The letter L," said the secretary, who was new to his job: "does that stand for Liberalism or liberality?"

Most of the recipients of Ministerial favour were expected to qualify in both of those subjects.

"Literature," explained the Minister.

And thus, after a fashion, Colonel Harrowcluff's expectation of seeing his son's name in the list of Honours was gratified.

THE YARKAND MANNER

SIR LULWORTH QUAYNE was making a leisurely progress through the Zoological Society's Gardens in company with his nephew, recently returned from Mexico. The latter was interested in comparing and contrasting allied types of animals occurring in the North American and Old World fauna.

"One of the most remarkable things in the wanderings of species," he observed, "is the sudden impulse to trek and migrate that breaks out now and again, for no apparent reason, in communities of hitherto stay-at-home animals."

"In human affairs the same phenomenon is occasionally noticeable," said Sir Lulworth; "perhaps the most striking instance of it occurred in this country while you were away in the wilds of Mexico. I mean the wander fever which suddenly displayed itself in the managing and editorial staffs of certain London newspapers. It began with the stampede of the entire staff of one of our most brilliant and enterprising weeklies to the banks of the Seine and the heights of Montmartre. The migration was a brief one, but it heralded an era of restlessness in the Press world which lent quite a new meaning to the phrase 'newspaper circulation.' Other editorial staffs were not slow to imitate the example that had been set them. Paris soon dropped out of fashion as being too near home; Nürnberg, Seville, and Salonica became more favoured as planting-out grounds for the personnel of not only weekly but daily papers as well. The localities were perhaps not always well chosen; the fact of a leading organ of Evangelical thought being edited for two successive fortnights from Trouville and Monte Carlo was generally admitted to have been a mistake. And even when enterprising and adventurous editors took themselves and their staffs further afield there were some unavoidable clashings. For instance, the *Scrutator*, *Sporting Bluff* and *The Damsels' Own Paper* all pitched on Khartoum for the same week. It was, perhaps, a desire to out-distance all possible competition that influenced the management of the *Daily Intelligencer*, one of the most solid and respected organs of Liberal opinion, in its decision to transfer its offices for three or four weeks from Fleet Street to Eastern Turkestan, allowing, of course, a necessary margin of time for the journey there and back. This was, in many respects, the most remarkable of all the Press stampedes that were experienced at this time. There was no make-believe about the undertaking; proprietor, manager, editor, sub-editors, leader-writers, principal reporters, and so forth, all took part in what was popularly alluded to as the *Drang nach Osten*; an intelligent and efficient office-boy was all that was left in the deserted hive of editorial industry."

"That was doing things rather thoroughly, wasn't it?" said the nephew.

"Well, you see," said Sir Lulworth, "the migration idea was falling somewhat into disrepute from the half-hearted manner in which it was occasionally carried out. You were not impressed by the information that such and such a paper was being edited and brought out at Lisbon or Innsbruck if you chanced to see the principal leader-writer or the art editor lunching as usual at their accustomed restaurants. The *Daily Intelligencer* was determined to give no loophole for cavil at the genuineness of its pilgrimage, and it must be admitted that to a certain extent the arrangements made for transmitting copy and carrying on the usual features of the paper during the long outward journey worked smoothly and well. The series of articles which commenced at Baku on 'What Cobdenism might do for the camel industry' ranks among the best of the recent contributions to Free Trade literature, while the views on foreign policy enunciated 'from a roof in Yarkand' showed at least as much grasp of the international situation as those that had germinated within half a mile of Downing Street. Quite in keeping, too, with the older and better traditions of British journalism was the manner of the home-coming; no bombast, no personal advertisement, no flamboyant interviews. Even a complimentary luncheon at the Voyagers' Club was courteously declined. Indeed, it began to be felt that the self-effacement of the returned pressmen was being carried to a pedantic length. Foreman compositors, advertisement clerks, and other members of the non-editorial staff, who had, of course, taken no part in the great trek, found it as impossible to get into direct communication with the editor and his satellites now that they had returned as when they had been excusably inaccessible in Central Asia. The sulky, overworked office-boy, who was the one connecting link between the editorial brain and the business departments of the paper, sardonically explained the new aloofness as the 'Yarkand manner.' Most of the reporters and sub-editors seemed to have been dismissed in autocratic fashion since their return and new ones engaged by letter; to these the editor and his immediate associates remained an unseen presence, issuing its instructions solely through the medium of curt type-written notes. Something mystic and Tibetan and forbidden had replaced the human bustle and democratic simplicity of pre-migration days, and the same experience was encountered by those who made social overtures to the returned wanderers. The most brilliant hostess of Twentieth Century London flung the pearl of her hospitality into the unresponsive trough of the editorial letter-box; it seemed as if nothing short of a Royal command would drag the hermit-souled *revenants* from their self-imposed seclusion. People began to talk unkindly of the effect of high altitudes and Eastern atmosphere on minds and temperaments unused to such luxuries. The Yarkand manner was not popular."

"And the contents of the paper," said the nephew, "did they show the influence of the new style?"

"Ah!" said Sir Lulworth, "that was the exciting thing. In home affairs, social questions, and the ordinary events of the day not much change was noticeable. A certain Oriental carelessness seemed to have crept into the editorial department, and perhaps a note of lassitude not unnatural in the work of men who had returned from what has been a fairly arduous journey. The aforetime standard of excellence was scarcely maintained, but at any rate the general lines of policy and outlook were not departed from. It was in the realm of foreign affairs that a startling change took place. Blunt, forcible, outspoken articles appeared, couched in language which nearly turned the autumn manœuvres of six important Powers into mobilizations. Whatever else the *Daily Intelligencer* had learned in the East, it had not acquired the art of diplomatic ambiguity. The man in the street enjoyed the articles and bought the paper as he had never bought it before; the men in Downing Street took a different view. The Foreign Secretary, hitherto accounted a rather reticent man, became positively garrulous in the course of perpetually disavowing the sentiments expressed in the *Daily Intelligencer's* leaders; and then one day the Government came to the conclusion that something definite and drastic must be done. A deputation, consisting of the Prime Minister, the Foreign Secretary, four leading financiers, and a well-known Nonconformist divine, made its way to the offices of the paper. At the door leading to the editorial department the way was barred by a nervous but defiant office-boy.

"'You can't see the editor nor any of the staff,'" he announced.

"'We insist on seeing the editor or some responsible person,' said the Prime Minister, and the deputation forced its way in. The boy had spoken truly; there was no one to be seen. In the whole suite of rooms there was no sign of human life.

"'Where is the editor?' 'Or the foreign editor,' 'Or the chief leader-writer?' 'Or anybody?'

"In answer to the shower of questions the boy unlocked a drawer and produced a strange-looking envelope, which bore a Khokand postmark, and a date of some seven or eight months back. It contained a scrap of paper on which was written the following message:

"'Entire party captured by brigand tribe on homeward journey. Quarter of million demanded as ransom, but would probably take less. Inform Government, relations, and friends.'

"There followed the signatures of the principal members of the party and instructions as to how and where the money was to be paid.

"The letter had been directed to the office-boy-in-charge, who had quietly suppressed it. No one is a hero to one's own office-boy, and he evidently considered that a quarter of a million was an unwarrantable outlay for such a doubtfully advantageous object as the repatriation of an errant newspaper staff. So he drew the editorial and other salaries, forged what signatures were necessary, engaged new reporters, did what sub-editing he could, and made as much use as possible of the large accumulation of special articles that was held in reserve for emergencies. The articles on foreign affairs were entirely his own composition.

"Of course the whole thing had to be kept as quiet as possible; an interim staff, pledged to secrecy, was appointed to keep the paper going till the pining captives could be sought out, ransomed, and brought home, in twos and threes to escape notice, and gradually things were put back on their old footing. The articles on foreign affairs reverted to the wonted traditions of the paper."

"But," interposed the nephew, "how on earth did the boy account to the relatives all those months for the non-appearance——"

"That," said Sir Lulworth, "was the most brilliant stroke of all. To the wife or nearest relative of each of the missing men he forwarded a letter, copying the handwriting of the supposed writer as well as he could, and making excuses about vile pens and ink; in each letter he told the same story, varying only the locality, to the effect that the writer, alone of the whole party, was unable to tear himself away from the wild liberty and allurements of Eastern life, and was going to spend several months roaming in some selected region. Many of the wives started off immediately in pursuit of their errant husbands, and it took the Government a considerable time and much trouble to reclaim them from their fruitless quests along the banks of the Oxus, the Gobi Desert, the Orenburg steppe, and other outlandish places. One of them, I believe, is still lost somewhere in the Tigris Valley."

"And the boy?"

"Is still in journalism."

THE BYZANTINE OMELETTE

SOPHIE CHATTEL-MONKHEIM was a Socialist by conviction and a Chattel-Monkheim by marriage. The particular member of that wealthy family whom she had married was rich, even as his relatives counted riches. Sophie had very advanced and decided views as to the distribution of money: it was a pleasing and fortunate circumstance that she also had the money. When she inveighed eloquently against the evils of capitalism at drawing-room meetings and Fabian conferences she was conscious of a comfortable feeling that the system, with all its inequalities and iniquities, would probably last her time. It is one of the consolations of middle-aged reformers that the good they inculcate must live after them if it is to live at all.

On a certain spring evening, somewhere towards the dinner-hour, Sophie sat tranquilly between her mirror and her maid, undergoing the process of having her hair built into an elaborate reflection of the prevailing fashion. She was hedged round with a great peace, the peace of one who has attained a desired end with much effort and perseverance, and who has found it still eminently desirable in its attainment. The Duke of Syria had consented to come beneath her roof as a guest, was even now installed beneath her roof, and would shortly be sitting at her dining-table. As a good Socialist, Sophie disapproved of social distinctions, and derided the idea of a princely caste, but if there were to be these artificial gradations of rank and dignity she was pleased and anxious to have an exalted specimen of an exalted order included in her house party. She was broad-minded enough to love the sinner while hating the sin—not that she entertained any warm feeling of personal affection for the Duke of Syria, who was a comparative stranger, but still, as Duke of Syria, he was very, very welcome beneath her roof. She could not have explained why, but no one was likely to ask her for an explanation, and most hostesses envied her.

"You must surpass yourself to-night, Richardson," she said complacently to her maid; "I must be looking my very best. We must all surpass ourselves."

The maid said nothing, but from the concentrated look in her eyes and the deft play of her fingers it was evident that she was beset with the ambition to surpass herself.

A knock came at the door, a quiet but peremptory knock, as of some one who would not be denied.

"Go and see who it is," said Sophie; "it may be something about the wine."

Richardson held a hurried conference with an invisible messenger at the door; when she returned there was noticeable a curious listlessness in place of her hitherto alert manner.

"What is it?" asked Sophie.

"The household servants have 'downed tools,' madame," said Richardson.

"Downed tools!" exclaimed Sophie; "do you mean to say they've gone on strike?"

"Yes, madame," said Richardson, adding the

information: "It's Gaspare that the trouble is about."

"Gaspare?" said Sophie wonderingly; "the emergency chef! The omelette specialist!"

"Yes, madame. Before he became an omelette specialist he was a valet, and he was one of the strike-breakers in the great strike at Lord Grimford's two years ago. As soon as the household staff here learned that you had engaged him they resolved to 'down tools' as a protest. They haven't got any grievance against you personally, but they demand that Gaspare should be immediately dismissed."

"But," protested Sophie, "he is the only man in England who understands how to make a Byzantine omelette. I engaged him specially for the Duke of Syria's visit, and it would be impossible to replace him at short notice. I should have to send to Paris, and the Duke loves Byzantine omelettes. It was the one thing we talked about coming from the station."

"He was one of the strike-breakers at Lord Grimford's," reiterated Richardson.

"This is too awful," said Sophie; "a strike of servants at a moment like this, with the Duke of Syria staying in the house. Something must be done immediately. Quick, finish my hair and I'll go and see what I can do to bring them round."

"I can't finish your hair, madame," said Richardson quietly, but with immense decision. "I belong to the union and I can't do another half-minute's work till the strike is settled. I'm sorry to be disobliging."

"But this is inhuman!" exclaimed Sophie tragically; "I've always been a model mistress and I've refused to employ any but union servants, and this is the result. I can't finish my hair myself; I don't know how to. What am I to do? It's wicked!"

"Wicked is the word," said Richardson; "I'm a good Conservative, and I've no patience with this Socialist foolery, asking your pardon. It's tyranny, that's what it is, all along the line, but I've my living to make, same as other people, and I've got to belong to the union. I couldn't touch another hair-pin without a strike permit, not if you was to double my wages."

The door burst open and Catherine Malsom raged into the room.

"Here's a nice affair," she screamed, "a strike of household servants without a moment's warning, and I'm left like this! I can't appear in public in this condition."

After a very hasty scrutiny Sophie assured her that she could not.

"Have they *all* struck?" she asked her maid.

"Not the kitchen staff," said Richardson, "they belong to a different union."

"Dinner at least will be assured," said Sophie, "that is something to be thankful for."

"Dinner!" snorted Catherine, "what on earth is the good of dinner when none of us will be able to appear at it? Look at your hair—and look at me! or rather, don't."

"I know it's difficult to manage without a maid; can't your husband be any help to you?" asked Sophie despairingly.

"Henry? He's in worse case than any of us. His man is the only person who really understands that ridiculous new-fangled Turkish bath that he insists on taking with him everywhere."

"Surely he could do without a Turkish bath for

one evening," said Sophie; "I can't appear without hair, but a Turkish bath is a luxury."

"My good woman," said Catherine, speaking with a fearful intensity, "Henry was *in* the bath when the strike started. *In* it, do you understand? He's there now."

"Can't he get out?"

"He doesn't know how to. Every time he pulls the lever marked 'release' he only releases hot steam. There are two kinds of steam in the bath, 'bearable' and 'scarcely bearable'; he has released them both. By this time I'm probably a widow."

"I simply can't send away Gaspare," wailed Sophie; "I should never be able to secure another omelette specialist."

"Any difficulty that I may experience in securing another husband is of course a trifle beneath anyone's consideration," said Catherine bitterly.

Sophie capitulated. "Go," she said to Richardson, "and tell the Strike Committee, or whoever are directing this affair, that Gaspare is herewith dismissed. And ask Gaspare to see me presently in the library, when I will pay him what is due to him and make what excuses I can; and then fly back and finish my hair."

Some half an hour later Sophie marshalled her guests in the Grand Salon preparatory to the formal march to the dining-room. Except that Henry Malsom was of the ripe raspberry tint that one sometimes sees at private theatricals representing the human complexion, there was little outward sign among those assembled of the crisis that had just been encountered and surmounted. But the tension had been too stupefying while it lasted not to leave some mental effects behind it. Sophie talked at random to her illustrious guest, and found her eyes straying with increasing frequency towards the great doors through which would presently come the blessed announcement that dinner was served. Now and again she glanced mirror-ward at the reflection of her wonderfully coiffed hair, as an insurance underwriter might gaze thankfully at an overdue vessel that had ridden safely into harbour in the wake of a devastating hurricane. Then the doors opened and the welcome figure of the butler entered the room. But he made no general announcement of a banquet in readiness, and the doors closed behind him; his message was for Sophie alone.

"There is no dinner, madame," he said gravely; "the kitchen staff have 'downed tools.' Gaspare belongs to the Union of Cooks and Kitchen Employees, and as soon as they heard of his summary dismissal at a moment's notice they struck work. They demand his instant reinstatement and an apology to the union. I may add, madame, that they are very firm; I've been obliged even to hand back the dinner rolls that were already on the table."

After the lapse of eighteen months Sophie Chattel-Monkheim is beginning to go about again among her old haunts and associates, but she still has to be very careful. The doctors will not let her attend anything at all exciting, such as a drawing-room meeting or a Fabian conference; it is doubtful, indeed, whether she wants to.

THE FEAST OF NEMESIS

"IT'S a good thing that Saint Valentine's Day has dropped out of vogue," said Mrs. Thackenbury; "what with Christmas and New Year and Easter, not to speak of birthdays, there are quite enough remembrance days as it is. I tried to save myself trouble at Christmas by just sending flowers to all my friends, but it wouldn't work; Gertrude has eleven hot-houses and about thirty gardeners, so it would have been ridiculous to send flowers to her, and Milly has just started a florist's shop, so it was equally out of the question there. The stress of having to decide in a hurry what to give to Gertrude and Milly just when I thought I'd got the whole question nicely off my mind completely ruined my Christmas, and then the awful monotony of the letters of thanks: 'Thank you so much for your lovely flowers. It was so good of you to think of me.' Of course in the majority of cases I hadn't thought about the recipients at all; their names were down in my list of 'people who must not be left out.' If I trusted to remembering them there would be some awful sins of omission."

"The trouble is," said Clovis to his aunt, "all these days of intrusive remembrance harp so persistently on one aspect of human nature and entirely ignore the other; that is why they become so perfunctory and artificial. At Christmas and New Year you are emboldened and encouraged by convention to send gushing messages of optimistic goodwill and servile affection to people whom you would scarcely ask to lunch unless some one else had failed you at the last moment; if you are supping at a restaurant on New Year's Eve you are permitted and expected to join hands and sing 'For Auld Lang Syne' with strangers whom you have never seen before and never want to see again. But no licence is allowed in the opposite direction."

"Opposite direction; what opposite direction?" queried Mrs. Thackenbury.

"There is no outlet for demonstrating your feelings towards people whom you simply loathe. That is really the crying need of our modern civilization. Just think how jolly it would be if a recognized day were set apart for the paying off of old scores and grudges, a day when one could lay oneself out to be gracefully vindictive to a carefully treasured list of 'people who must not be let off.' I remember when I was at a private school we had one day, the last Monday of the term I think it was, consecrated to the settlement of feuds and grudges; of course we did not appreciate it as much as it deserved, because after all, any day of the term could be used for that purpose. Still, if one had chastised a smaller boy for being cheeky weeks before, one was always permitted on that day to recall the episode to his memory by chastising him again. That is what the French call reconstructing the crime."

"I should call it reconstructing the punishment," said Mrs. Thackenbury; "and, anyhow, I don't see how you could introduce a system of primitive schoolboy vengeance into civilized adult life. We haven't outgrown our passions, but we are supposed to have learned how to keep them within strictly decorous limits."

"Of course the thing would have to be done furtively and politely," said Clovis; "the charm of it would be that it would never be perfunctory like the other thing. Now, for instance, you say to yourself: 'I must show the Webleys some attention at Christmas, they were kind to dear Bertie at Bournemouth,' and you send them a calendar, and daily for six days after Christmas the male Webley asks the female Webley if she has remembered to thank you for the calendar you sent them. Well, transplant that idea to the other and more human side of your nature, and say to yourself: 'Next Thursday is Nemesis Day; what on earth can I do to those odious people next door who made such an absurd fuss when Ping Yang bit their youngest child?' Then you'd get up awfully early on the allotted day and climb over into their garden and dig for truffles on their tennis court with a good gardening fork, choosing, of course, that part of the court that was screened from observation by the laurel bushes. You wouldn't find any truffles but you would find a great peace, such as no amount of present-giving could ever bestow."

"I shouldn't," said Mrs. Thackenbury, though her air of protest sounded a bit forced; "I should feel rather a worm for doing such a thing."

"You exaggerate the power of upheaval which a worm would be able to bring into play in the limited time available," said Clovis; "if you put in a strenuous ten minutes with a really useful fork, the result ought to suggest the operations of an unusually masterful mole or a badger in a hurry."

"They might guess I had done it," said Mrs. Thackenbury.

"Of course they would," said Clovis; "that would be half the satisfaction of the thing, just as you like people at Christmas to know what presents or cards you've sent them. The thing would be much easier to manage, of course, when you were on outwardly friendly terms with the object of your dislike. That greedy little Agnes Blaik, for instance, who thinks of nothing but her food, it would be quite simple to ask her to a picnic in some wild woodland spot and lose her just before lunch was served; when you found her again every morsel of food could have been eaten up."

"It would require no ordinary human strategy to lose Agnes Blaik when luncheon was imminent: in fact, I don't believe it could be done."

"Then have all the other guests, people whom you dislike, and lose the luncheon. It could have been sent by accident in the wrong direction."

"It would be a ghastly picnic," said Mrs. Thackenbury.

"For them, but not for you," said Clovis; "you would have had an early and comforting lunch before you started, and you could improve the occasion by mentioning in detail the items of the missing banquet—the lobster Newburg and the egg mayonnaise, and the curry that was to have been heated in a chafing-dish. Agnes Blaik would be delirious long before you got to the list of wines, and in the long interval of waiting, before they had quite abandoned hope of the lunch turning up, you could induce them to play silly games, such as that idiotic one of 'the Lord Mayor's dinner-party,' in which every one has to choose the name of a dish and do something futile when it is called out In this case they would probably burst into tears when their dish is mentioned. It would be a heavenly picnic."

Mrs. Thackenbury was silent for a moment ; she was probably making a mental list of the people she would like to invite to the Duke Humphrey picnic. Presently she asked : " And that odious young man, Waldo Plubley, who is always coddling himself—have you thought of anything that one could do to him ?" Evidently she was beginning to see the possibilities of Nemesis Day.

" If there was anything like a general observance of the festival," said Clovis, " Waldo would be in such demand that you would have to bespeak him weeks beforehand, and even then, if there were an east wind blowing or a cloud or two in the sky he might be too careful of his precious self to come out. It would be rather jolly if you could lure him into a hammock in the orchard, just near the spot where there is a wasps' nest every summer. A comfortable hammock on a warm afternoon would appeal to his indolent tastes, and then, when he was getting drowsy, a lighted fusee thrown into the nest would bring the wasps out in an indignant mass, and they would soon find a 'home away from home' on Waldo's fat body. It takes some doing to get out of a hammock in a hurry."

"They might sting him to death," protested Mrs. Thackenbury.

"Waldo is one of those people who would be enormously improved by death," said Clovis ; " but if you didn't want to go as far as that, you could have some wet straw ready to hand, and set it alight under the hammock at the same time that the fusee was thrown into the nest; the smoke would keep all but the most militant of the wasps just outside the stinging line, and as long as Waldo remained within its protection he would escape serious damage, and could be eventually restored to his mother, kippered all over and swollen in places, but still perfectly recognizable."

"His mother would by my enemy for life," said Mrs. Thackenbury.

"That would be one greeting less to exchange at Christmas," said Clovis.

THE DREAMER

IT was the season of sales. The august establishment of Walpurgis and Nettlepink had lowered its prices for an entire week as a concession to trade observances, much as an Archduchess might protestingly contract an attack of influenza for the unsatisfactory reason that influenza was locally prevalent. Adela Chemping, who considered herself in some measure superior to the allurements of an ordinary bargain sale, made a point of attending the reduction week at Walpurgis and Nettlepink's.

" I'm not a bargain hunter," she said, " but I like to go where bargains are."

Which showed that beneath her surface strength of character there flowed a gracious undercurrent of human weakness.

With a view to providing herself with a male escort Mrs. Chemping had invited her youngest nephew to accompany her on the first day of the shopping expedition, throwing in the additional allurement of a cinematograph theatre and the prospect of light refreshment. As Cyprian was not yet eighteen, she hoped he might not have reached that stage in masculine development when parcel-carrying is looked on as a thing abhorrent.

" Meet me just outside the floral department," she wrote to him, " and don't be a moment later than eleven."

Cyprian was a boy who carried with him through early life the wondering look of a dreamer, the eyes of one who sees things that are not visible to ordinary mortals, and invests the commonplace things of this world with qualities unsuspected by plainer folk—the eyes of a poet or a house agent. He was quietly dressed—that sartorial quietude which frequently accompanies early adolescence, and is usually attributed by novel-writers to the influence of a widowed mother. His hair was brushed back in a smoothness as of ribbon seaweed and seamed with a narrow furrow that scarcely aimed at being a parting. His aunt particularly noted this item of his toilet when they met at the appointed rendezvous, because he was standing waiting for her bareheaded.

"Where is your hat?" she asked.

"I didn't bring one with me," he replied.

Adela Chemping was slightly scandalized.

"You are not going to be what they call a Nut, are you?" she inquired with some anxiety, partly with the idea that a Nut would be an extravagance which her sister's small household would scarcely be justified in incurring, partly, perhaps, with the instinctive apprehension that a Nut, even in its embryo stage, would refuse to carry parcels.

Cyprian looked at her with his wondering, dreamy eyes.

"I didn't bring a hat," he said, "because it is such a nuisance when one is shopping; I mean it is so awkward if one meets anyone one knows and has to take one's hat off when one's hands are full of parcels. If one hasn't got a hat on one can't take it off."

Mrs. Chemping sighed with great relief; her worst fear had been laid at rest.

"It is more orthodox to wear a hat," she observed, and then turned her attention briskly to the business in hand.

"We will go first to the table-linen counter," she said, leading the way in that direction; "I should like to look at some napkins."

The wondering look deepened in Cyprian's eyes as he followed his aunt; he belonged to a generation that is supposed to be over-fond of the rôle of mere spectator, but looking at napkins that one did not mean to buy was a pleasure beyond his comprehension. Mrs. Chemping held one or two napkins up to the light and stared fixedly at them, as though she half expected to find some revolutionary cypher written on them in scarcely visible ink; then she suddenly broke away in the direction of the glass-ware department.

"Millicent asked me to get her a couple of decanters if there were any going really cheap," she explained on the way, "and I really do want a salad bowl. I can come back to the napkins later on."

She handled and scrutinized a large number of decanters and a long series of salad bowls, and finally bought seven chrysanthemum vases.

"No one uses that kind of vase nowadays," she informed Cyprian, "but they will do for presents next Christmas."

Two sunshades that were marked down to a price that Mrs. Chemping considered absurdly cheap were added to her purchases.

"One of them will do for Ruth Colson; she is going out to the Malay States, and a sunshade will always be useful there. And I must get her some thin writing paper. It takes up no room in one' baggage."

Mrs. Chemping bought stacks of writing paper it was so cheap, and it went so flat in a trunk or portmanteau. She also bought a few envelopes—envelopes somehow seemed rather an extravagance compared with notepaper.

"Do you think Ruth will like blue or grey paper?" she asked Cyprian.

"Grey," said Cyprian, who had never met the lady in question.

"Have you any mauve notepaper of this quality?" Adela asked the assistant.

"We haven't any mauve," said the assistant, "but we've two shades of green and a darker shade of grey."

Mrs. Chemping inspected the greens and the darker grey, and chose the blue.

"Now we can have some lunch," she said.

Cyprian behaved in an exemplary fashion in the refreshment department, and cheerfully accepted a fish cake and a mince pie and a small cup of coffee as adequate restoratives after two hours of concentrated shopping. He was adamant, however, in resisting his aunt's suggestion that a hat should be bought for him at the counter where men's head-wear was being disposed of at temptingly reduced prices.

"I've got as many hats as I want at home," he said, "and besides, it rumples one's hair so, trying them on."

Perhaps he was going to develop into a Nut after all. It was a disquieting symptom that he left all the parcels in charge of the cloak-room attendant.

"We shall be getting more parcels presently,"

e said, "so we need not collect these till we have nished our shopping."

His aunt was doubtfully appeased; some of the leasure and excitement of a shopping expedition eemed to evaporate when one was deprived of immediate personal contact with one's purchases.

"I'm going to look at those napkins again," she aid, as they descended the stairs to the ground floor. 'You need not come," she added, as the dreaming ook in the boy's eyes changed for a moment into ne of mute protest, "you can meet me afterwards in he cutlery department; I've just remembered that I haven't a corkscrew in the house that can be depended on."

Cyprian was not to be found in the cutlery department when his aunt in due course arrived there, but in the crush and bustle of anxious shoppers and busy attendants it was an easy matter to miss anyone. It was in the leather goods department some quarter of an hour later that Adela Chemping caught sight of her nephew, separated from her by a rampart of suitcases and portmanteaux and hemmed in by the jostling crush of human beings that now invaded every corner of the great shopping emporium. She was just in time to witness a pardonable but rather embarrassing mistake on the part of a lady who had wriggled her way with unstayable determination towards the bareheaded Cyprian, and was now breathlessly demanding the sale price of a handbag which had taken her fancy.

"There now," exclaimed Adela to herself, "she takes him for one of the shop assistants because he hasn't got a hat on. I wonder it hasn't happened before."

Perhaps it had. Cyprian, at any rate, seemed neither startled nor embarrassed by the error into which the good lady had fallen. Examining the ticket on the bag, he announced in a clear, dispassionate voice :

" Black seal, thirty-four shillings marked down to twenty-eight. As a matter of fact, we are clearing them out at a special reduction price of twenty-six shillings. They are going off rather fast."

" I'll take it," said the lady, eagerly digging some coins out of her purse.

" Will you take it as it is ? " asked Cyprian ; " it will be a matter of a few minutes to get it wrapped up, there is such a crush."

" Never mind, I'll take it as it is," said the purchaser, clutching her treasure and counting the money into Cyprian's palm.

Several kind strangers helped Adela into the open air.

" It's the crush and the heat," said one sympathiser to another ; " it's enough to turn anyone giddy."

When she next came across Cyprian he was standing in the crowd that pushed and jostled around the counters of the book department. The dream look was deeper than ever in his eyes. He had just sold two books of devotion to an elderly Canon.

THE QUINCE TREE

"I'VE just been to see old Betsy Mullen," announced Vera to her aunt, Mrs. Bebberly Cumble; "she seems in rather a bad way about her rent. She owes about fifteen weeks of it, and says she doesn't know where any of it is to come from."

"Betsy Mullen always is in difficulties with her rent, and the more people help her with it the less she troubles about it," said the aunt. "I certainly am not going to assist her any more. The fact is, she will have to go into a smaller and cheaper cottage; there are several to be had at the other end of the village for half the rent that she is paying, or supposed to be paying, now. I told her a year ago that she ought to move."

"But she wouldn't get such a nice garden anywhere else," protested Vera, "and there's such a jolly quince tree in the corner. I don't suppose there's another quince tree in the whole parish. And she never makes any quince jam; I think to have a quince tree and not to make quince jam shows such strength of character. Oh, she can't possibly move away from that garden."

"When one is sixteen," said Mrs. Bebberly Cumble severely, "one talks of things being impossible which are merely uncongenial. It is not only possible but it is desirable that Betsy Mullen should move into smaller quarters; she has scarcely enough furniture to fill that big cottage."

"As far as value goes," said Vera after a short pause, "there is more in Betsy's cottage than in any other house for miles round."

"Nonsense," said the aunt; "she parted with whatever old china ware she had long ago."

"I'm not talking about anything that belongs to Betsy herself," said Vera darkly; "but of course, you don't know what I know, and I don't suppose I ought to tell you."

"You must tell me at once," exclaimed the aunt, her senses leaping into alertness like those of a terrier suddenly exchanging a bored drowsiness for the lively anticipation of an immediate rat hunt.

"I'm perfectly certain that I oughtn't to tell you anything about it," said Vera, "but, then, I often do things that I oughtn't to do."

"I should be the last person to suggest that you should do anything that you ought not to do——" began Mrs. Bebberly Cumble impressively.

"And I am always swayed by the last person who speaks to me," admitted Vera, "so I'll do what I ought not to do and tell you."

Mrs. Bebberley Cumble thrust a very pardonable sense of exasperation into the background of her mind and demanded impatiently:

"What is there in Betsy Mullen's cottage that you are making such a fuss about?"

"It's hardly fair to say that *I've* made a fuss about it," said Vera; "this is the first time I've mentioned the matter, but there's been no end of trouble and mystery and newspaper speculation about it. It's rather amusing to think of the columns of conjecture in the Press and the police and detectives hunting about everywhere at home and abroad, and all the while that innocent-looking little cottage has held the secret."

"You don't mean to say it's the Louvre picture, La Something or other, the woman with the smile, that disappeared about two years ago?" exclaimed the aunt with rising excitement.

"Oh no, not that," said Vera, "but something quite as important and just as mysterious—if anything, rather more scandalous."

"Not the Dublin——?"

Vera nodded.

"The whole jolly lot of them."

"In Betsy's cottage? Incredible!"

"Of course Betsy hasn't an idea as to what they are," said Vera; "she just knows that they are something valuable and that she must keep quiet about them. I found out quite by accident what they were and how they came to be there. You see, the people who had them were at their wits' end to know where to stow them away for safe keeping, and some one who was motoring through the village was struck by the snug loneliness of the cottage and thought it would be just the thing. Mrs. Lamper arranged the matter with Betsy and smuggled the things in."

"Mrs. Lamper?"

"Yes; she does a lot of district visiting, you know."

"I am quite aware that she takes soup and flannel and improving literature to the poorer cottages," said Mrs. Bebberly Cumble, "but that is hardly the same sort of thing as disposing of stolen goods, and she must have known something about their history; anyone who reads the papers, even casually, must have been aware of the theft, and I should think the things were not hard to recognize. Mrs. Lamper has always had the reputation of being a very conscientious woman."

"Of course she was screening some one else," said Vera. "A remarkable feature of the affair is the extraordinary number of quite respectable people who have involved themselves in its meshes by trying to shield others. You would be really astonished if you knew some of the names of the individuals mixed up in it, and I don't suppose a tithe of them knew who the original culprits were; and now I've got you entangled in the mess by letting you into the secret of the cottage."

"You most certainly have not entangled me," said Mrs. Bebberly Cumble indignantly. "I have no intention of shielding anybody. The police must know about it at once; a theft is a theft, whoever is involved. If respectable people choose to turn themselves into receivers and disposers of stolen goods, well, they've ceased to be respectable, that's all. I shall telephone immediately——"

"Oh, aunt," said Vera reproachfully, "it would break the poor Canon's heart if Cuthbert were to be involved in a scandal of this sort. You know it would."

"Cuthbert involved! How can you say such things when you know how much we all think of him?"

"Of course I know you think a lot of him, and that he's engaged to marry Beatrice, and that it will be a frightfully good match, and that he's your ideal of what a son-in-law ought to be. All the same, it was Cuthbert's idea to stow the things away in the cottage, and it was his motor that brought them. He was only doing it to help his freind Pegginson, you know—the Quaker man, who is always agitating for a smaller Navy. I forget how he got involved in it. I warned you that there were lots of quite respectable people mixed up in it, didn't I? That's what I meant when I said it would be impossible for old Betsy to leave the cottage; the things take up a good bit of room, and she couldn't go carrying them about with her other goods and chattels without attracting notice. Of course if she were to fall ill and die it would be equally unfortunate. Her mother lived to be over ninety, she tells me, so with due care and an absence of worry she ought to last for another dozen years at least. By that time perhaps some other arrangements will have been made for disposing of the wretched things."

"I shall speak to Cuthbert about it—after the wedding," said Mrs. Bebberly Cumble.

. . .

"The wedding isn't till next year," said Vera, in recounting the story to her best girl friend, "and meanwhile old Betsy is living rent free, with soup twice a week and my aunt's doctor to see her whenever she has a finger ache."

"But how on earth did you get to know about it all?" asked her friend, in admiring wonder.

"It was a mystery——" said Vera.

"Of course it was a mystery, a mystery that baffled everybody. What beats me is how you found out——"

"Oh, about the jewels? I invented that part," explained Vera; "I mean the mystery was where old Betsy's arrears of rent were to come from; and she would have hated leaving that jolly quince tree."

THE FORBIDDEN BUZZARDS

"IS matchmaking at all in your line?"

Hugo Peterby asked the question with a certain amount of personal interest.

"I don't specialize in it," said Clovis; "it's all right while you're doing it, but the after-effects are sometimes so disconcerting—the mute reproachful looks of the people you've aided and abetted in matrimonial experiments. It's as bad as selling a man a horse with half a dozen latent vices and watching him discover them piecemeal in the course of the hunting season. I suppose you're thinking of the Coulterneb girl. She's certainly jolly, and quite all right as far as looks go, and I believe a certain amount of money adheres to her. What I don't see is how you will ever manage to propose to her. In all the time I've known her I don't remember her to have stopped talking for three consecutive minutes. You'll have to race her six times round the grass paddock for a bet, and then blurt your proposal out before she's got her wind back. The paddock is laid up for hay, but if you're really in love with her you won't let a consideration of that sort stop you, especially as it's not your hay."

"I think I could manage the proposing part right enough," said Hugo, "if I could count on being left alone with her for four or five hours. The trouble is that I'm not likely to get anything like that amount of grace. That fellow Lanner is showing signs of interesting himself in the same quarter. He's quite heartbreakingly rich and is rather a swell in his way; in fact, our hostess is obviously a bit flattered at having him here. If she gets wind of the fact that he's inclined to be attracted by Betty Coulterneb she'll think it a splendid match and throw them into each other's arms all day long, and then where will my opportunities come in? My one anxiety is to keep him out of the girl's way as much as possible, and if you could help me——"

"If you want me to trot Lanner round the countryside, inspecting alleged Roman remains and studying local methods of bee culture and crop raising, I'm afraid I can't oblige you," said Clovis. "You see, he's taken something like an aversion to me since the other night in the smoking-room."

"What happened in the smoking-room?"

"He trotted out some well-worn chestnut as the latest thing in good stories, and I remarked, quite innocently, that I never could remember whether it was George II. or James II. who was so fond of that particular story, and now he regards me with politely-draped dislike. I'll do my best for you, if the opportunity arises, but it will have to be in a roundabout, impersonal manner."

. . . .

"It's so nice having Mr. Lanner here," confided Mrs. Olston to Clovis the next afternoon; "he's always been engaged when I've asked him before. Such a nice man; he really ought to be married to some nice girl. Between you and me, I have an idea that he came down here for a certain reason."

"I've had much the same idea," said Clovis,

lowering his voice; "in fact, I'm almost certain of it."

"You mean he's attracted by——" began Mrs. Olston eagerly.

"I mean he's here for what he can get," said Clovis.

"For what he can *get*?" said the hostess with a touch of indignation in her voice; "what do you mean? He's a very rich man. What should he want to get here?"

"He has one ruling passion," said Clovis, "and there's something he can get here that is not to be had for love nor for money anywhere else in the country, as far as I know."

"But what? Whatever do you mean? What is his ruling passion?"

"Egg-collecting," said Clovis. "He has agents all over the world getting rare eggs for him, and his collection is one of the finest in Europe; but his great ambition is to collect his treasures personally. He stops at no expense nor trouble to achieve that end."

"Good heavens! The buzzards, the rough-legged buzzards!" exclaimed Mrs. Olston; "you don't think he's going to raid their nest?"

"What do you think yourself?" asked Clovis; "the only pair of rough-legged buzzards known to breed in this country are nesting in your woods. Very few people know about them, but as a member of the league for protecting rare birds that information would be at his disposal. I came down in the train with him, and I noticed that a bulky volume of Dresser's *Birds of Europe* was one of the requisites that he had packed in his travelling-kit. It was the volume dealing with short-winged hawks and buzzards."

Clovis believed that if a lie was worth telling it was worth telling well.

"This is appalling," said Mrs. Olston; "my husband would never forgive me if anything happened to those birds. They've been seen about the woods for the last year or two, but this is the first time they've nested. As you say, they are almost the only pair known to be breeding in the whole of Great Britain; and now their nest is going to be harried by a guest staying under my roof. I must do something to stop it. Do you think if I appealed to him——?"

Clovis laughed.

"There is a story going about, which I fancy is true in most of its details, of something that happened not long ago somewhere on the coast of the Sea of Marmora, in which our friend had a hand. A Syrian nightjar, or some such bird, was known to be breeding in the olive gardens of a rich Armenian, who for some reason or other wouldn't allow Lanner to go in and take the eggs though he offered cash down for the permission. The Armenian was found beaten nearly to death a day or two later, and his fences levelled. It was assumed to be a case of Mussulman aggression, and noted as such in all the Consular reports, but the eggs are in the Lanner collection. No, I don't think I should appeal to his better feelings if I were you."

"I must do something," said Mrs. Olston tearfully; my husband's parting words when he went off to Norway were an injunction to see that those birds were not disturbed, and he's asked about them every time he's written. Do suggest something."

"I was going to suggest picketing," said Clovis.

"Picketing! You mean setting guards round the birds?"

"No; round Lanner. He can't find his way through those woods by night, and you could arrange that you or Evelyn or Jack or the German governess should be by his side in relays all day long. A fellow guest he could get rid of, but he couldn't very well shake off members of the household, and even the most determined collector would hardly go climbing after forbidden buzzards' eggs with a German governness hanging round his neck, so to speak."

Lanner, who had been lazily watching for an opportunity for prosecuting his courtship of the Coulterneb girl, found presently that his chances of getting her to himself for ten minutes even were non-existent. If the girl was ever alone he never was. His hostess had changed suddenly, as far as he was concerned, from the desirable type that lets her guests do nothing in the way that best pleases them, to the sort that drags them over the ground like so many harrows. She showed him the herb garden and the greenhouses, the village church, some water-colour sketches that her sister had done in Corsica, and the place where it was hoped that celery would grow later in the year. He was shown all the Aylesbury ducklings and the row of wooden hives where there would have been bees if there had not been bee disease. He was also taken to the end of a long lane and shown a distant mound whereon local tradition reported that the Danes had once pitched a camp. And when his hostess had to desert him temporarily for other duties he would find Evelyn walking solemnly by his side. Evelyn was fourteen and talked chiefly about good and evil, and of how much one might accomplish in the way of regenerating the world if one was thoroughly determined to do one's utmost. It was generally rather a relief when she was displaced by Jack, who was nine years old, and talked exclusively about the Balkan War without throwing any fresh light on its political or military history. The German governess told Lanner more about Schiller than he had ever heard in his life about any one person; it was perhaps his own fault for having told her that he was not interested in Goethe. When the governess went off picket duty the hostess was again on hand with a not-to-be-gainsaid invitation to visit the cottage of an old woman who remembered Charles James Fox; the woman had been dead for two or three years. but the cottage was still there. Lanner was called back to town earlier than he had originally intended.

Hugo did not bring off his affair with Betty Coulterneb. Whether she refused him or whether, as was more generally supposed, he did not get a chance of saying three consecutive words, has never been exactly ascertained. Anyhow, she is still the jolly Coulterneb girl.

The buzzards successfully reared two young ones, which were shot by a local hairdresser.

THE STAKE

"RONNIE is a great trial to me," said Mrs. Attray plaintively. "Only eighteen years old last February and already a confirmed gambler. I am sure I don't know where he inherits it from; his father never touched cards, and you know how little I play—a game of bridge on Wednesday afternoons in the winter, for threepence a hundred, and even that I shouldn't do if it wasn't that Edith always wants a fourth and could be certain to ask that detestable Jenkinham woman if she couldn't get me. I would much rather sit and talk any day than play bridge; cards are such a waste of time, I think. But as to Ronnie, bridge and baccarat and poker-patience are positively all that he thinks about. Of course I've done my best to stop it; I've asked the Norridrums not to let him play cards when he's over there, but you might as well ask the Atlantic Ocean to keep quiet for a crossing as expect them to bother about a mother's natural anxieties."

"Why do you let him go there?" asked Eleanor Saxelby.

"My dear," said Mrs. Attray, "I don't want to offend them. After all, they are my landlords and I have to look to them for anything I want done about the place; they were very accommodating about the new roof for the orchid house. And they lend me one of their cars when mine is out of order; you know how often it gets out of order."

"I don't know how often," said Eleanor, "but it must happen very frequently. Whenever I want you to take me anywhere in your car I am always told that there is something wrong with it, or else that that the chauffeur has got neuralgia and you don't like to ask him to go out."

"He suffers quite a lot from neuralgia," said Mrs. Attray hastily. "Anyhow," she continued, "you can understand that I don't want to offend the Norridrums. Their household is the most rackety one in the county, and I believe no one ever knows to an hour or two when any particular meal will appear on the table or what it will consist of when it does appear."

Eleanor Saxelby shuddered. She liked her meals to be of regular occurrence and assured proportions.

"Still," pursued Mrs. Attray, "whatever their own home life may be, as landlords and neighbours they are considerate and obliging, so I don't want to quarrel with them. Besides, if Ronnie didn't play cards there he'd be playing somewhere else."

"Not if you were firm with him," said Eleanor; "I believe in being firm."

"Firm? I am firm," exclaimed Mrs. Attray; "I am more than firm—I am farseeing. I've done everything I can think of it to prevent Ronnie from playing for money. I've stopped his allowance for the rest of the year, so he can't even gamble on credit, and I've subscribed a lump sum to the church offertory in his name instead of giving him instalments of small silver to put in the bag on Sundays. I wouldn't even let him have the money to tip the hunt servants with, but sent it by postal order. He was furiously sulky about it, but I reminded him of what happened to the ten shillings that I gave him for the Young Men's Endeavour League 'Self-Denial Week.'"

"What did happen to it?" asked Eleanor.

"Well, Ronnie did some preliminary endeavouring with it, on his own account, in connection with the Grand National. If it had come off, as he expressed it, he would have given the League twenty-five shillings and netted a comfortable commission for himself; as it was, that ten shillings was one of the things the League had to deny itself. Since then I've been careful not to let him have a penny piece in his hands."

"He'll get round that in some way," said Eleanor with quiet conviction; "he'll sell things."

"My dear, he's done all that is to be done in that direction already. He's got rid of his wrist-watch and his hunting flask and both his cigarette cases, and I shouldn't be surprised if he's wearing imitation-gold sleeve links instead of those his Aunt Rhoda gave him on his seventeenth birthday. He can't sell his clothes, of course, except his winter overcoat, and I've locked that up in the camphor cupboard on the pretext of preserving it from moth. I really don't see what else he can raise money on. I consider that I've been both firm and farseeing."

"Has he been at the Norridrums lately?" asked Eleanor.

"He was there yesterday afternoon and stayed to dinner," said Mrs. Attray. "I don't quite know when he came home, but I fancy it was late."

"Then depend on it he was gambling," said Eleanor, with the assured air of one who has few ideas and makes the most of them. "Late hours in the country always mean gambling."

"He can't gamble if he has no money and no chance of getting any," argued Mrs. Attray; "even if one plays for small stakes one must have a decent prospect of paying one's losses."

"He may have sold some of the Amherst pheasant chicks," suggested Eleanor; "they would fetch about ten or twelve shillings each, I dare say."

"Ronnie wouldn't do such a thing," said Mrs. Attray; "and anyhow I went and counted them this morning and they're all there. No," she continued, with the quiet satisfaction that comes from a sense of painstaking and merited achievement, "I fancy that Ronnie had to content himself with the rôle of onlooker last night, as far as the card-table was concerned."

"Is that clock right?" asked Eleanor, whose eyes had been straying restlessly towards the mantel-piece for some little time; "lunch is usually so punctual in your establishment."

"Three minutes past the half-hour," exclaimed Mrs. Attray; "cook must be preparing something unusually sumptuous in your honour. I am not in the secret; I've been out all the morning, you know."

Eleanor smiled forgivingly. A special effort by Mrs. Attray's cook was worth waiting a few minutes for.

As a matter of fact, the luncheon fare, when it made its tardy appearance, was distinctly unworthy of the reputation which the justly-treasured cook had built up for herself. The soup alone would have sufficed to cast a gloom over any meal that it had inaugurated, and it was not redeemed by anything that followed. Eleanor said little, but when she spoke there was a hint of tears in her voice that was far more eloquent than outspoken denunciation would have been, and even the insouciant Ronald showed traces of depression when he tasted the rognons Saltikoff.

"Not quite the best luncheon I've enjoyed in your house," said Eleanor at last, when her final hope had flickered out with the savoury.

"My dear, it's the worst meal I've sat down to for years," said her hostess; "that last dish tasted principally of red pepper and wet toast. I'm awfully sorry. Is anything the matter in the kitchen, Pellin?" she asked of the attendant maid.

"Well, ma'am, the new cook hadn't hardly time to see to things properly, coming in so sudden——" commenced Pellin by way of explanation.

"The *new* cook!" screamed Mrs. Attray.

"Colonel Norridrum's cook, ma'am," said Pellin.

"What on earth do you mean? What is Colonel Norridrum's cook doing in my kitchen—and where is *my* cook?"

"Perhaps I can explain better than Pellin can," said Ronald hurriedly; "the fact is, I was dining at the Norridrums' yesterday, and they were wishing they had a swell cook like yours, just for to-day and to-morrow, while they've got some gourmet staying with them; their own cook is no earthly good—well, you've seen what she turns out when she's at all flurried. So I thought it would be rather sporting to play them at baccarat for the loan of our cook against a money stake, and I lost, that's all. I have had rotten luck at baccarat all this year."

The remainder of his explanation, of how he had assured the cooks that the temporary transfer had his mother's sanction, and had smuggled the one out and the other in during the maternal absence, was drowned in the outcry of scandalized upbraiding.

"If I had sold the woman into slavery there couldn't have been a bigger fuss about it," he confided afterwards to Bertie Norridrum, "and Eleanor Saxelby raged and ramped the louder of the two. I tell you what, I'll bet you two of the Amherst pheasants to five shillings that she refuses to have me as a partner at the croquet tournament. We're drawn together, you know."

This time he won his bet.

CLOVIS ON PARENTAL RESPONSIBILITIES

MARION EGGELBY sat talking to Clovis on the only subject that she ever willingly talked about—her offspring and their varied perfections and accomplishments. Clovis was not in what could be called a receptive mood; the younger generation of Eggelby, depicted in the glowing improbable colours of parent impressionism, aroused in him no enthusiasm. Mrs. Eggelby, on the other hand, was furnished with enthusiasm enough for two.

"You would like Eric," she said, argumentatively rather than hopefully. Clovis had intimated very unmistakably that he was unlikely to care extravagantly for either Amy or Willie. "Yes, I feel sure you would like Eric. Every one takes to him at once. You know, he always reminds me of that famous picture of the youthful David—I forget who it's by, but it's very well known."

"That would be sufficient to set me against him, if I saw much of him," said Clovis. "Just imagine at auction bridge, for instance, when one was trying to concentrate one's mind on what one's partner's original declaration had been, and to remember what suits one's opponents had originally discarded, what it would be like to have some one persistently reminding one of a picture of the youthful David. It would be simply maddening. If Eric did that I should detest him."

"Eric doesn't play bridge," said Mrs. Eggelby with dignity.

"Doesn't he?" asked Clovis; "why not?"

"None of my children have been brought up to play card games," said Mrs. Eggelby; "draughts and halma and those sorts of games I encourage. Eric is considered quite a wonderful draughts-player."

"You are strewing dreadful risks in the path of your family," said Clovis; "a friend of mine who is a prison chaplain told me that among the worst criminal cases that have come under his notice, men condemned to death or to long periods of penal servitude, there was not a single bridge-player. On the other hand, he knew at least two expert draughts-players among them."

"I really don't see what my boys have got to do with the criminal classes," said Mrs. Eggelby resentfully. "They have been most carefully brought up, I can assure you that."

"That shows that you were nervous as to how they would turn out," said Clovis. "Now, my mother never bothered about bringing me up. She just saw to it that I got whacked at decent intervals and was taught the difference between right and wrong; there is some difference, you know, but I've forgotten what it is."

"Forgotten the difference between right and wrong!" exclaimed Mrs. Eggelby.

"Well, you see, I took up natural history and a whole lot of other subjects at the same time, and one can't remember everything, can one? I used to know the difference between the Sardinian dormouse and the ordinary kind, and whether the wryneck arrives at our shores earlier than the cuckoo, or the other way round, and how long the walrus takes in growing to maturity; I dare say you knew all those sorts of thing once, but I bet you've forgotten them."

"Those things are not important," said Mrs. Eggelby, "but——"

"The fact that we've both forgotten them proves that they *are* important," said Clovis; "you must have noticed that it's always the important things that one forgets, while the trivial, unnecessary facts of life stick in one's memory. There's my cousin, Editha Clubberley, for instance; I can never forget that her birthday is on the 12th of October. It's a matter of utter indifference to me on what date her birthday falls, or whether she was born at all; either fact seems to me absolutely trivial, or unnecessary—I've heaps of other cousins to go on with. On the other hand, when I'm staying with Hildegarde Shrubley I can never remember the important circumstance whether her first husband got his unenviable reputation on the Turf or the Stock Exchange, and that uncertainty rules Sport and Finance out of the conversation at once. One can never mention travel, either, because her second husband had to live permanently abroad."

"Mrs. Shrubley and I move in very different circles," said Mrs. Eggelby stiffly.

"No one who knows Hildegarde could possibly accuse her of moving in a circle," said Clovis; "her view of life seems to be a non-stop run with an inexhaustible supply of petrol. If she can get some one else to pay for the petrol so much the better. I don't mind confessing to you that she has taught me more than any other woman I can think of."

"What kind of knowledge?" demanded Mrs. Eggelby, with the air a jury might collectively wear when finding a verdict without leaving the box.

"Well, among other things, she's introduced me to at least four different ways of cooking lobster," said Clovis gratefully. "That, of course, wouldn't appeal to you; people who abstain from the pleasures of the card-table never really appreciate the finer possibilities of the dining-table. I suppose their powers of enlightened enjoyment get atrophied from disuse."

"An aunt of mine was very ill after eating a lobster," said Mrs. Eggelby.

"I dare say, if we knew more of her history, we should find out that she'd often been ill before eating the lobster. Aren't you concealing the fact that she'd had measles and influenza and nervous headache and hysteria, and other things that aunts do have, long before she ate the lobster? Aunts that have never known a day's illness are very rare; in fact, I don't personally know of any. Of course if she ate it as a child of two weeks old it might have been her first illness—and her last. But if that was the case I think you should have said so."

"I must be going," said Mrs. Eggelby, in a tone which had been thoroughly sterilized of even perfunctory regret.

Clovis rose with an air of graceful reluctance.

"I have so enjoyed our little talk about Eric," he said; "I quite look forward to meeting him some day."

"Good-bye," said Mrs. Eggelby frostily; the supplementary remark which she made at the back of her throat was——

"I'll take care that you never shall!"

A HOLIDAY TASK

KENELM JERTON entered the dining-hall of the Golden Galleon Hotel in the full crush of the luncheon hour. Nearly every seat was occupied, and small additional tables had been brought in, where floor space permitted, to accommodate late-comers, with the result that many of the tables were almost touching each other. Jerton was beckoned by a waiter to the only vacant table that was discernible, and took his seat with the uncomfortable and wholly groundless idea that nearly every one in the room was staring at him. He was a youngish man of ordinary appearance, quiet of dress and unobtrusive of manner, and he could never wholly rid himself of the idea that a fierce light of public scrutiny beat on him as though he had been a notability or a super-nut. After he had ordered his lunch there came the unavoidable interval of waiting, with nothing to do but to stare at the flower-vase on his table and to be stared at (in imagination) by several flappers, some maturer beings of the same sex, and a satirical-looking Jew. In order to carry off the situation with some appearance of unconcern he became spuriously interested in the contents of the flower-vase.

"What is the name of those roses, d'you know?" he asked the waiter. The waiter was ready at all times to conceal his ignorance concerning items of the wine-list or *menu*; he was frankly ignorant as to the specific name of the roses.

"*Amy Silvester Partington*," said a voice at Jerton's elbow.

The voice came from a pleasant-faced, well-dressed young woman who was sitting at a table that almost touched Jerton's. He thanked her hurriedly and nervously for the information, and made some inconsequent remark about the flowers.

"It is a curious thing," said the young woman, "that I should be able to tell you the name of those roses without an effort of memory, because if you were to ask me my name I should be utterly unable to give it to you."

Jerton had not harboured the least intention of extending his thirst for name-labels to his neighbour. After her rather remarkable announcement, however, he was obliged to say something in the way of polite inquiry.

"Yes," answered the lady, "I suppose it is a case of partial loss of memory. I was in the train coming down here; my ticket told me that I had come from Victoria and was bound for this place. I had a couple of five-pound notes and a sovereign on me, no visiting cards or any other means of identification, and no idea as to who I am. I can only hazily recollect that I have a title; I am Lady Somebody—beyond that my mind is a blank."

"Hadn't you any luggage with you?" asked Jerton.

"That is what I didn't know. I knew the name of this hotel and made up my mind to come here, and when the hotel porter who meets the trains asked if I had any luggage I had to invent a dressing-bag and dress-basket; I could always pretend that they had gone astray. I gave him the name of Smith, and presently he emerged from a confused pile of luggage and passengers with a dressing-bag and dress-basket labelled Kestrel-Smith. I had to take them ; I don't see what else I could have done."

Jerton said nothing, but he rather wondered what the lawful owner of the baggage would do.

"Of course it was dreadful arriving at a strange hotel with the name of Kestrel-Smith, but it would have been worse to have arrived without luggage. Anyhow, I hate causing trouble."

Jerton had visions of harassed railway officials and distraught Kestrel-Smiths, but he made no attempt to clothe his mental picture in words. The lady continued her story.

"Naturally, none of my keys would fit the things, but I told an intelligent page boy that I had lost my key-ring, and he had the locks forced in a twinkling. Rather too intelligent, that boy ; he will probably end in Dartmoor. The Kestrel-Smith toilet tools aren't up to much, but they are better than nothing."

"If you feel sure that you have a title," said Jerton, "why not get hold of a peerage and go right through it?"

"I tried that. I skimmed through the list of the House of Lords in 'Whitaker,' but a mere printed string of name conveys awfully little to one, you know. If you were an army officer and had lost your identity you might pore over the Army List for months without finding out who you were. I'm going on another tack ; I'm trying to find out by various little tests who I am *not*—that will narrow the range of uncertainty down a bit. You may have noticed, for instance, that I'm lunching principally off lobster Newburg."

Jerton had not ventured to notice anything of the sort.

"It's an extravagance, because it's one of the most expensive dishes on the *menu*, but at any rate it proves that I'm not Lady Starping; she never touches shell-fish, and poor Lady Braddleshrub has no digestion at all; if I am *her* I shall certainly die in agony in the course of the afternoon, and the duty of finding out who I am will devolve on the press and the police and those sort of people; I shall be past caring. Lady Knewford doesn't know one rose from another and she hates men, so she wouldn't have spoken to you in any case; and Lady Mousehilton flirts with every man she meets—I haven't flirted with you, have I?"

Jerton hastily gave the required assurance.

"Well, you see," continued the lady, "that knocks four off the list at once."

"It'll be rather a lengthy process bringing the list down to one," said Jerton.

"Oh, but, of course, there are heaps of them that I couldn't possibly be—women who've got grandchildren or sons old enough to have celebrated their coming of age. I've only got to consider the ones about my own age. I tell you how you might help me this afternoon, if you don't mind; go through any of the back numbers of *Country Life* and those sort of papers that you can find in the smoking-room, and see if you come across my portrait with infant son or anything of that sort. It won't take you ten minutes. I'll meet you in the lounge about tea-time. Thanks awfully."

And the Fair Unknown, having graciously pressed Jerton into the search for her lost identity, rose and left the room. As she passed the young man's table she halted for a moment and whispered:

"Did you notice that I tipped the waiter a shilling? We can cross Lady Ulwight off the list; she would have died rather than do that."

At five o'clock Jerton made his way to the hotel lounge; he had spent a diligent but fruitless quarter of an hour among the illustrated weeklies in the smoking-room. His new acquaintance was seated at a small tea-table, with a waiter hovering in attendance.

"China tea or Indian?" she asked as Jerton came up.

"China, please, and nothing to eat. Have you discovered anything?"

"Only negative information. I'm not Lady Befnal. She disapproves dreadfully at any form of gambling, so when I recognized a well-known book-maker in the hotel lobby I went and put a tenner on an unnamed filly by William the Third out of Mitrovitza for the three-fifteen race. I suppose the fact of the animal being nameless was what attracted me."

"Did it win?" asked Jerton.

"No, came in fourth, the most irritating thing a horse can do when you've backed it win or place. Anyhow, I know now that I'm not Lady Befnal."

"It seems to me that the knowledge was rather dearly bought," commented Jerton.

"Well, yes, it has rather cleared me out," admitted the identity-seeker; "a florin is about all I've got left on me. The lobster Newburg made my lunch rather an expensive one, and, of course, I had to tip that boy for what he did to the Kestrel-Smith locks. I've got rather a useful idea, though. I feel certain that I belong to the Pivot Club; I'll go back to town and ask the hall porter there if there are any etters for me. He knows all the members by sight, and if there are any letters or telephone messages waiting for me of course that will solve the problem. If he says there aren't any, I shall say : 'You know who I am, don't you ?' so I'll find out anyway."

The plan seemed a sound one ; a difficulty in its execution suggested itself to Jerton.

"Of course," said the lady, when he hinted at the obstacle, "there's my fare back to town, and my bill here and cabs and things. If you'll lend me three pounds that ought to see me through comfortably. Thanks ever so. Then there is the question of that luggage : I don't want to be saddled with that for the rest of my life. I'll have it brought down to the hall and you can pretend to mount guard over it while I'm writing a letter. Then I shall just slip away to the station, and you can wander off to the smoking-room, and they can do what they like with the things. They'll advertise them after a bit and the owner can claim them."

Jerton acquiesced in the manœuvre, and duly mounted guard over the luggage while its temporary owner slipped unobtrusively out of the hotel. Her departure was not, however, altogether unnoticed. Two gentlemen were strolling past Jerton, and one of them remarked to the other :

"Did you see that tall young woman in grey who went out just now ? She is the Lady——"

His promenade carried him out of earshot at the critical moment when he was about to disclose the elusive identity. The Lady Who ? Jerton could scarcely run after a total stranger, break into his conversation, and ask him for information concerning a chance passer-by. Besides, it was desirable that he should keep up the appearance of looking after the luggage. In a minute or two, however, the important personage, the man who knew, came strolling back alone. Jerton summoned up all his courage and waylaid him.

"I think I heard you say you knew the lady who went out of the hotel a few minutes ago, a tall lady, dressed in grey. Excuse me for asking if you could tell me her name; I've been talking to her for half an hour; she—er—she knows all my people and seems to know me, so I suppose I've met her somewhere before, but I'm blest if I can put a name to her. Could you——?"

"Certainly. She's a Mrs. Stroope"

"*Mrs.?*" queried Jerton.

"Yes, she's the Lady Champion at golf in my part of the world. An awful good sort, and goes about a good deal in Society, but she has an awkward habit of losing her memory every now and then, and gets into all sorts of fixes. She's furious, too, if you make any allusion to it afterwards. Good day, sir."

The stranger passed on his way, and before Jerton had had time to assimilate his information he found his whole attention centred on an angry-looking lady who was making loud and fretful-seeming inquiries of the hotel clerks.

"Has any luggage been brought here from the station by mistake, a dress-basket and dressing-case, with the name Kestrel-Smith? It can't be traced anywhere. I saw it put in at Victoria, that I'll swear. Why—there *is* my luggage! and the locks have been tampered with!"

Jerton heard no more. He fled down to the Turkish bath, and stayed there for hours.

THE STALLED OX

THEOPHIL ESHLEY was an artist by profession, a cattle painter by force of environment. It is not to be supposed that he lived on a ranch or a dairy farm, in an atmosphere pervaded with horn and hoof, milking-stool, and branding-iron. His home was in a park-like, villa-dotted district that only just escaped the reproach of being suburban. On one side of his garden there abutted a small, picturesque meadow, in which an enterprising neighbour pastured some small picturesque cows of the Channel Island persuasion. At noonday in summertime the cows stood knee-deep in tall meadow-grass under the shade of a group of walnut trees, with the sunlight falling in dappled patches on their mouse-sleek coats. Eshley had conceived and executed a dainty picture of two reposeful milch-cows in a setting of walnut-tree and meadow-grass and filtered sunbeam, and the Royal Academy had duly exposed the same on the walls of its Summer Exhibition. The Royal Academy encourages orderly, methodical habits in its children. Eshley had painted a successful and acceptable picture of cattle drowsing picturesquely under walnut trees, and as he had begun, so, of necessity, he went on. His "Noontide Peace," a study of two dun cows under a walnut tree, was followed by "A Mid-day Sanctuary," a study of a walnut tree, with two dun cows under it. In due succession there came "Where the Gad-Flies Cease from Troubling," "The Haven of the Herd," and "A Dream in Dairyland," studies of walnut trees and dun cows. His two attempts to break away from his own tradition were signal failures "Turtle Doves alarmed by Sparrow-hawk" and "Wolves on the Roman Campagna" came back to his studio in the guise of abominable heresies, and Eshley climbed back into grace and the public gaze with "A Shaded Nook where Drowsy Milkers Dream."

On a fine afternoon in late autumn he was putting some finishing touches to a study of meadow weeds when his neighbour, Adela Pingsford, assailed the outer door of his studio with loud peremptory knockings.

"There is an ox in my garden," she announced, in explanation of the tempestuous intrusion.

"An ox," said Eshley blankly, and rather fatuously; "what kind of ox?"

"Oh, I don't know what kind," snapped the lady. "A common or garden ox, to use the slang expression. It is the garden part of it that I object to. My garden has just been put straight for the winter, and an ox roaming about in it won't improve matters. Besides, there are the chrysanthemums just coming into flower."

"How did it get into the garden?" asked Eshley.

"I imagine it came in by the gate," said the lady impatiently; "it couldn't have climbed the walls, and I don't suppose anyone dropped it from an areoplane as a Bovril advertisement. The immediately important question is not how it got in, but how to get it out."

"Won't it go?" said Eshley

"If it was anxious to go," said Adela Pingsford ather angrily, "I should not have come here to chat vith you about it. I'm practically all alone; the ousemaid is having her afternoon out and the cook s lying down with an attack of neuralgia. Anyhing that I may have learned at school or in after ife about how to remove a large ox from a small garden seems to have escaped from my memory now. All I could think of was that you were a near neighbour and a cattle painter, presumably more or less familiar with the subjects that you painted, and that you might be of some slight assistance. Possibly I was mistaken."

"I paint dairy cows, certainly," admitted Eshley, "but I cannot claim to have had any experience in rounding up stray oxen. I've seen it done on a cinema film, of course, but there were always horses and lots of other accessories; besides, one never knows how much of those pictures are faked."

Adela Pingsford said nothing, but led the way to her garden. It was normally a fair-sized garden, but it looked small in comparison with the ox, a huge mottled brute, dull red about the head and shoulders, passing to dirty white on the flanks and hind-quarters, with shaggy ears and large blood-shot eyes. It bore about as much resemblance to the dainty paddock heifers that Eshley was accustomed to paint as the chief of a Kurdish nomad clan would to a Japanese tea-shop girl. Eshley stood very near the gate while he studied the animal's appearance and demeanour. Adela Pingsford continued to say nothing.

"It's eating a chrysanthemum," said Eshley at last, when the silence had become unbearable.

"How observant you are," said Adela bitterly.

"You seem to notice everything. As a matter of fact, it has got six chrysanthemums in its mouth at the present moment."

The necessity for doing something was becoming imperative. Eshley took a step or two in the direction of the animal, clapped his hands, and made noises of the "Hish" and "Shoo" variety. If the ox heard them it gave no outward indication of the fact.

"If any hens should ever stray into my garden," said Adela, "I should certainly send for you to frighten them out. You 'shoo' beautifully. Meanwhile, do you mind trying to drive that ox away? That is a *Mademoiselle Louise Bichot* that he's begun on now," she added in icy calm, as a glowing orange head was crushed into the huge munching mouth.

"Since you have been so frank about the variety of the chrysanthemum," said Eshley, "I don't mind telling you that this is an Ayrshire ox."

The icy calm broke down; Adela Pingsford used language that sent the artist instinctively a few feet nearer to the ox. He picked up a pea-stick and flung it with some determination against the animal's mottled flanks. The operation of mashing *Mademoiselle Louis Bichot* into a petal salad was suspended for a long moment, while the ox gazed with concentrated inquiry at the stick-thrower. Adela gazed with equal concentration and more obvious hostility at the same focus. As the beast neither lowered its head nor stamped its feet Eshley ventured on another javelin exercise with another pea-stick. The ox seemed to realize at once that it was to go; it gave a hurried final pluck at the bed where the chrysanthemums had been, and strode swiftly up the garden. Eshley ran to head it towards the gate, but nly succeeded in quickening its pace from a walk o a lumbering trot. With an air of inquiry, but with o real hesitation, it crossed the tiny strip of turf hat the charitable called the croquet lawn, and pushed ts way through the open French window into the norning-room. Some chrysanthemums and other utumn herbage stood about the room in vases, and the animal resumed its browsing operations ; all the same, Eshley fancied that the beginnings of a hunted look had come into its eyes, a look that counselled respect. He discontinued his attempt to interfere with its choice of surroundings.

"Mr. Eshley," said Adela in a shaking voice, "I asked you to drive that beast out of my garden, but I did not ask you to drive it into my house. If I must have it anywhere on the premises I prefer the garden to the morning-room."

"Cattle drives are not in my line," said Eshley ; "if I remember I told you so at the outset."

"I quite agree," retorted the lady, "painting pretty pictures of pretty little cows is what you're suited for. Perhaps you'd like to do a nice sketch of that ox making itself at home in my morning-room ?"

This time it seemed as if the worm had turned ; Eshley began striding away.

"Where are you going ?" screamed Adela.

"To fetch implements," was the sanwer.

"Implements ? I won't have you use a lasso. The room will be wrecked if there's a struggle."

But the artist marched out of the garden. In a couple of minutes he returned, laden with easel, sketching-stool, and painting materials.

"Do you mean to say that you're going to sit

quietly down and paint that brute while it's destroying my morning-room?" gasped Adela.

"It was your suggestion," said Eshley, setting his canvas in position.

"I forbid it; I absolutely forbid it!" stormed Adela.

"I don't see what standing you have in the matter," said the artist; "you can hardly pretend that it's your ox, even by adoption."

"You seem to forget that it's in my morning-room, eating my flowers," came the raging retort.

"You seem to forget that the cook has neuralgia," said Eshley; "she may be just dozing off into a merciful sleep and your outcry will waken her. Consideration for others should be the guiding principle of people in our station of life."

"The man is mad!" exclaimed Adela tragically. A moment later it was Adela herself who appeared to go mad. The ox had finished the vase-flowers and the cover of "Israel Kalisch," and appeared to be thinking of leaving its rather restricted quarters. Eshley noticed its restlessness and promptly flung it some bunches of Virginia creeper leaves as an inducement to continue the sitting.

"I forget how the proverb runs," he observed; "something about 'better a dinner of herbs than a stalled ox where hate is.' We seem to have all the ingredients for the proverb ready to hand."

"I shall go to the Public Library and get them to telephone for the police," announced Adela, and, raging audibly, she departed.

Some minutes later the ox, awakening probably to the suspicion that oil cake and chopped mangold was waiting for it in some appointed byre, stepped with much precaution out of the morning-room, stared with grave inquiry at the no longer obtrusive and pea-stick-throwing human, and then lumbered heavily but swiftly out of the garden. Eshley packed up his tools and followed the animal's example and "Larkdene" was left to neuralgia and the cook.

The episode was the turning-point in Eshley's artistic career. His remarkable picture, "Ox in a morning-room, late autumn," was one of the sensations and successes of the next Paris Salon, and when it was subsequently exhibited at Munich it was bought by the Bavarian Government, in the teeth of the spirited bidding of three meat-extract firms. From that moment his success was continuous and assured, and the Royal Academy was thankful, two years later, to give a conspicuous position on its walls to his large canvas "Barbary Apes Wrecking a Boudoir."

Eshley presented Adela Pingsford with a new copy of "Israel Kalisch," and a couple of finely flowering plants of *Madame André Blusset*, but nothing in the nature of a real reconciliation has taken place between them.

THE STORY-TELLER

IT was a hot afternoon, and the railway carriage was correspondingly sultry, and the next stop was at Templecombe, nearly an hour ahead. The occupants of the carriage were a small girl, and a smaller girl, and a small boy. An aunt belonging to the children occupied one corner seat, and the further corner seat on the opposite side was occupied by a bachelor who was a stranger to their party, but the small girls and the small boy emphatically occupied the compartment. Both the aunt and the children were conversational in a limited, persistent way, reminding one of the attentions of a housefly that refused to be discouraged. Most of the aunt's remarks seemed to begin with "Don't," and nearly all of the children's remarks began with "Why?" The bachelor said nothing out loud.

"Don't, Cyril, don't," exclaimed the aunt, as the small boy began smacking the cushions of the seat, producing a cloud of dust at each blow.

"Come and look out of the window," she added.

The child moved reluctantly to the window. "Why are those sheep being driven out of that field?" he asked.

"I expect they are being driven to another field where there is more grass," said the aunt weakly.

"But there is lots of grass in that field," protested the boy ; "there's nothing else but grass there. Aunt, there's lots of grass in that field."

"Perhaps the grass in the other field is better," suggested the aunt fatuously.

"Why is it better?" came the swift, inevitable question.

"Oh, look at those cows!" exclaimed the aunt. Nearly every field along the line had contained cows or bullocks, but she spoke as though she were drawing attention to a rarity.

"Why is the grass in the other field better?" persisted Cyril.

The frown on the bachelor's face was deepening to a scowl. He was a hard, unsympathetic man, the aunt decided in her mind. She was utterly unable to come to any satisfactory decision about the grass in the other field.

The smaller girl created a diversion by beginning to recite "On the Road to Mandalay." She only knew the first line, but she put her limited knowledge to the fullest possible use. She repeated the line over and over again in a dreamy but resolute and very audible voice ; it seemed to the bachelor as though some one had had a bet with her that she could not repeat the line aloud two thousand times without stopping. Whoever it was who had made the wager was likely to lose his bet.

"Come over here and listen to a story," said the aunt, when the bachelor had looked twice at her and once at the communication cord.

The children moved listlessly towards the aunt's end of the carriage. Evidently her reputation as a story-teller did not rank high in their estimation.

In a low, confidential voice, interrupted at frequent intervals by loud, petulant questions from her listeners, she began an unenterprising and deplorably uninteresting story about a little girl who was good, and made friends with every one on account of her goodness, and was finally saved from a mad bull by a number of rescuers who admired her moral character.

"Wouldn't they have saved her if she hadn't been good?" demanded the bigger of the small girls. It was exactly the question that the bachelor had wanted to ask.

"Well, yes," admitted the aunt lamely, "but I don't think they would have run quite so fast to her help if they had not liked her so much."

"It's the stupidest story I've ever heard," said the bigger of the small girls, with immense conviction.

"I didn't listen after the first bit, it was so stupid," said Cyril.

The smaller girl made no actual comment on the story, but she had long ago recommenced a murmured repetition of her favourite line.

"You don't seem to be a success as a story-teller," said the bachelor suddenly from his corner.

The aunt bristled in instant defence at this unexpected attack.

"It's a very difficult thing to tell stories that children can both understand and appreciate," she said stiffly.

"I don't agree with you," said the bachelor.

"Perhaps *you* would like to tell them a story," was the aunt's retort.

"Tell us a story," demanded the bigger of the small girls.

"Once upon a time," began the bachelor, "there was a little girl called Bertha, who was extraordinarily good."

The children's momentarily-aroused interest began at once to flicker; all stories seemed dreadfully alike, no matter who told them.

"She did all that she was told, she was always truthful, she kept her clothes clean, ate milk puddings as though they were jam tarts, learned her lessons perfectly, and was polite in her manners."

"Was she pretty?" asked the bigger of the small girls.

"Not as pretty as any of you," said the bachelor, "but she was horribly good."

There was a wave of reaction in favour of the story; the word horrible in connection with goodness was a novelty that commended itself. It seemed to introduce a ring of truth that was absent from the aunt's tales of infant life.

"She was so good," continued the bachelor, "that she won several medals for goodness, which she always wore, pinned on to her dress. There was a medal for obedience, another medal for punctuality, and a third for good behaviour. They were large metal medals and they clicked against one another as she walked. No other child in the town where she lived had as many as three medals, so everybody knew that she must be an extra good child."

"Horribly good," quoted Cyril.

"Everybody talked about her goodness, and the Prince of the country got to hear about it, and he said that as she was so very good she might be allowed once a week to walk in his park, which was just outside the town. It was a beautiful park, and no children were ever allowed in it, so it was a great honour for Bertha to be allowed to go there."

"Were there any sheep in the park?" demanded Cyril.

"No," said the bachelor, "there were no sheep."

"Why weren't there any sheep?" came the inevitable question arising out of that answer.

The aunt permitted herself a smile, which might almost have been described as a grin.

"There were no sheep in the park," said the bachelor, "because the Prince's mother had once had a dream that her son would either be killed by a sheep or else by a clock falling on him. For that reason the Prince never kept a sheep in his park or a clock in his palace."

The aunt suppressed a gasp of admiration.

"Was the Prince killed by a sheep or by a clock?" asked Cyril.

"He is still alive, so we can't tell whether the dream will come true," said the bachelor unconcernedly; "anyway, there were no sheep in the park, but there were lots of little pigs running all over the place."

"What colour were they?"

"Black with white faces, white with black spots, black all over, grey with white patches, and some were white all over."

The story-teller paused to let a full idea of the park's treasures sink into the children's imaginations; then he resumed:

"Bertha was rather sorry to find that there were no flowers in the park. She had promised her aunts, with tears in her eyes, that she would not pick any of the kind Prince's flowers, and she had meant to keep her promise, so of course it made her feel silly to find that there were no flowers to pick."

"Why weren't there any flowers?"

"Because the pigs had eaten them all," said the bachelor promptly. "The gardeners had told the Prince that you couldn't have pigs and flowers, so he decided to have pigs and no flowers."

There was a murmur of approval at the excellence of the Prince's decision; so many people would have decided the other way.

"There were lots of other delightful things in the park. There were ponds with gold and blue and green fish in them, and trees with beautiful parrots that said clever things at a moment's notice, and humming birds that hummed all the popular tunes of the day. Bertha walked up and down and enjoyed herself immensely, and thought to herself: 'If I were not so extraordinarily good I should not have been allowed to come into this beautiful park and enjoy all that there is to be seen in it,' and her three medals clinked against one another as she walked and helped to remind her how very good she really was. Just then an enormous wolf came prowling into the park to see if it could catch a fat little pig for its supper."

"What colour was it?" asked the children, amid an immediate quickening of interest.

"Mud-colour all over, with a black tongue and pale grey eyes that gleamed with unspeakable ferocity. The first thing that it saw in the park was Bertha; her pinafore was so spotlessly white and clean that it could be seen from a great distance. Bertha saw the wolf and saw that it was stealing towards her, and she began to wish that she had never been allowed to come into the park. She ran as hard as she could, and the wolf came after her with huge leaps and bounds. She managed to reach a shrubbery of myrtle bushes and she hid herself in one of the thickets of the bushes. The wolf came sniffing among the branches, its black tongue lolling out of its mouth and its pale grey eyes glaring with rage. Bertha was terribly frightened, and thought to herself: 'If I had not been so extraordinarily good I should have been safe in the town at this moment.' However, the scent of the myrtle was so strong that the wolf could not sniff out where Bertha was hiding, and the bushes were so thick that he might have hunted about in them for a long time without catching sight of her, so he thought he might as well go off and catch a little pig instead. Bertha was trembling very much at having the wolf prowling and sniffing so near her, and as she trembled the medal for obedience clinked against the medals for good conduct and punctuality. The wolf was just moving away when he heard the sound of the medals clinking and stopped to listen; they clinked again in a bush quite near him. He dashed into the bush, his pale grey eyes gleaming with ferocity and triumph, and dragged Bertha out and devoured her to the last morsel. All that was left of her were her shoes, bits of clothing, and the three medals for goodness."

"Were any of the little pigs killed?"

"No, they all escaped."

"The story began badly," said the smaller of the small girls, "but it had a beautiful ending."

"It is the most beautiful story that I ever heard," said the bigger of the small girls, with immense decision.

"It is the *only* beautiful story I have ever heard," said Cyril.

A dissentient opinion came from the aunt.

"A most improper story to tell to young children! You have undermined the effect of years of careful teaching."

"At any rate," said the bachelor, collecting his belongings preparatory to leaving the carriage, "I kept them quiet for ten minutes, which was more than you were able to do."

"Unhappy woman!" he observed to himself as he walked down the platform of Templecombe station; "for the next six months or so those children will assail her in public with demands for an improper story!"

A DEFENSIVE DIAMOND

TREDDLEFORD sat in an easeful arm-chair in front of a slumberous fire, with a volume of verse in his hand and the comfortable consciousness that outside the club windows the rain was dripping and pattering with persistent purpose. A chill, wet October afternoon was emerging into a black, wet October evening, and the club smoking-room seemed warmer and cosier by contrast. It was an afternoon on which to be wafted away from one's climatic surroundings, and *The Golden Journey to Samarkand* promised to bear Treddleford well and bravely into other lands and under other skies. He had already migrated from London the rain-swept to Bagdad the Beautiful, and stood by the Sun Gate "in the olden time" when an icy breath of imminent annoyance seemed to creep between the book and himself. Amblecope, the man with the restless, prominent eyes and the mouth ready mobilized for conversational openings, had planted himself in a neighbouring arm-chair. For a twelvemonth and some odd weeks Treddleford had skilfully avoided making the acquaintance of his voluble fellow-clubman; he had marvellously escaped from the infliction of his relentless record of tedious personal achievements, or alleged achievements, on golf links, turf, and gaming table, by flood and field and covert-side. Now his season of immunity was coming to an end. There was no escape; in another moment he would be numbered among those who knew Amblecope to speak to—or rather, to suffer being spoken to.

The intruder was armed with a copy of *Country Life*, not for purposes of reading, but as an aid to conversational ice-breaking.

"Rather a good portrait of Throstlewing," he remarked explosively, turning his large challenging eyes on Treddleford; "somehow it reminds me very much of Yellowstep, who was supposed to be such a good thing for the Grand Prix in 1903. Curious race that was; I suppose I've seen every race for the Grand Prix for the last——"

"Be kind enough never to mention the Grand Prix in my hearing," said Treddleford desperately; "it awakens acutely distressing memories. I can't explain why without going into a long and complicated story."

"Oh, certainly, certainly," said Amblecope hastily; long and complicated stories that were not told by himself were abominable in his eyes. He turned the pages of *Country Life* and became spuriously interested in the picture of a Mongolian pheasant.

"Not a bad representation of the Mongolian variety," he exclaimed, holding it up for his neighbour's inspection. "They do very well in some covers. Take some stopping too once they're fairly on the wing. I suppose the biggest bag I ever made in two successive days——"

"My aunt, who owns the greater part of Lincolnshire," broke in Treddleford, with dramatic abruptness, "possesses perhaps the most remarkable record in the way of a pheasant bag that has ever been achieved. She is seventy-five and can't hit a thing, but she always goes out with the guns. When I say she can't hit a thing, I don't mean to say that she doesn't occasionally endanger the lives of her fellow-guns, because that wouldn't be true. In fact, the chief Government Whip won't allow Ministerial M.P.'s to go out with her; 'We don't want to incur by-elections needlessly,' he quite reasonably observed. Well, the other day she winged a pheasant, and brought it to earth with a feather or two knocked out of it; it was a runner, and my aunt saw herself in danger of being done out of about the only bird she'd hit during the present reign. Of course she wasn't going to stand that; she followed it through bracken and brushwood, and when it took to the open country and started across a ploughed field she jumped on to the shooting pony and went after it. The chase was a long one, and when my aunt at last ran the bird to a standstill she was nearer home than she was to the shooting party; she had left that some five miles behind her."

"Rather a long run for a wounded pheasant," snapped Amblecope.

"The story rests on my aunt's authority," said Treddleford coldly, "and she is local vice-president of the Young Women's Christian Association. She trotted three miles or so to her home, and it was not till the middle of the afternoon that it was discovered that the lunch for the entire shooting party was in a pannier attached to the pony's saddle. Anyway, she got her bird."

"Some birds, of course, take a lot of killing," said Amblecope; "so do some fish. I remember once I was fishing in the Exe, lovely trout stream, lots of fish, though they don't run to any great size——"

"One of them did," announced Treddleford, with

emphasis. "My uncle, the Bishop of Southmolton, came across a giant trout in a pool just off the main stream of the Exe near Ugworthy; he tried it with every kind of fly and worm every day for three weeks without an atom of success, and then Fate intervened on his behalf. There was a low stone bridge just over this pool, and on the last day of his fishing holiday a motor van ran violently into the parapet and turned completely over; no one was hurt, but part of the parapet was knocked away, and the entire load that the van was carrying was pitched over and fell a little way into the pool. In a couple of minutes the giant trout was flapping and twisting on bare mud at the bottom of a waterless pool, and my uncle was able to walk down to him and fold him to his breast. The van-load consisted of blotting-paper, and every drop of water in that pool had been sucked up into the mass of spilt cargo."

There was silence for nearly half a minute in the smoking-room, and Treddleford began to let his mind steal back towards the golden road that led to Samarkand. Amblecope, however, rallied, and remarked in a rather tired and dispirited voice:

"Talking of motor accidents, the narrowest squeak I ever had was the other day, motoring with old Tommy Yarby in North Wales. Awfully good sort, old Yarby, thorough good sportsman, and the best——"

"It was in North Wales," said Treddleford, "that my sister met with her sensational carriage accident last year. She was on her way to a garden-party at Lady Nineveh's, about the only garden-party that ever comes to pass in those parts in the course of the year, and therefore a thing that she would have been very sorry to miss. She was driving a young horse that she'd only bought a week or two previously, warranted to be perfectly steady with motor traffic, bicycles, and other common objects of the roadside. The animal lived up to its reputation, and passed the most explosive of motor-bikes with an indifference that almost amounted to apathy. However, I suppose we all draw the line somewhere, and this particular cob drew it at travelling wild beast shows. Of course my sister didn't know that, but she knew it very distinctly when she turned a sharp corner and found herself in a mixed company of camels, piebald horses, and canary-coloured vans. The dogcart was overturned in a ditch and kicked to splinters, and the cob went home across country. Neither my sister nor the groom was hurt, but the problem of how to get to the Nineveh garden-party, some three miles distant, seemed rather difficult to solve ; once there, of course, my sister would easily find some one to drive her home. 'I suppose you wouldn't care for the loan of a couple of my camels ?' the showman suggested, in humorous sympathy. 'I would,' said my sister, who had ridden camel-back in Egypt, and she overruled the objections of the groom, who hadn't. She picked out two of the most presentable-looking of the beasts and had them dusted and made as tidy as was possible at short notice, and set out for the Nineveh mansion. You may imagine the sensation that her small but imposing caravan created when she arrived at the hall door. The entire garden-party flocked up to gape. My sister was rather glad to slip down from her camel, and the groom was thankful to scramble down from his. Then young Billy Doulton, of the Dragoon Guards, who has been a lot at Aden and thinks he knows camel-language backwards, thought he would show off by making the beasts kneel down in orthodox fashion. Unfortunately camel words-of-command are not the same all the world over; these were magnificent Turkestan camels, accustomed to stride up the stony terraces of mountain passes, and when Doulton shouted at them they went side by side up the front steps, into the entrance hall, and up the grand staircase. The German governess met them just at the turn of the corridor. The Ninevehs nursed her with devoted attention for weeks, and when I last heard from them she was well enough to go about her duties again, but the doctor says she will always suffer from Hagenbeck heart."

Amblecope got up from his chair and moved to another part of the room. Treddleford reopened his book and betook himself once more across

> The dragon-green, the luminous, the dark, the serpent-haunted sea.

For a blessed half-hour he disported himself in imagination by the "gay Aleppo-Gate," and listened to the bird-voiced singing-man. Then the world of to-day called him back; a page summoned him to speak with a friend on the telephone.

As Treddleford was about to pass out of the room he encountered Amblecope, also passing out, on his way to the billiard-room, where, perchance, some luckless wight might be secured and held fast to listen to the number of his attendances at the Grand Prix, with subsequent remarks on Newmarket and the Cambridgeshire. Amblecope made as if to pass out first, but a new-born pride was surging in Treddleford's breast and he waved him back.

"I believe I take precedence," he said coldly; "you are merely the club Bore; I am the club Liar."

THE ELK

TERESA, Mrs. Thropplestance, was the richest and most intractable old woman in the county of Woldshire. In her dealings with the world in general her manner suggested a blend between a Mistress of the Robes and a Master of Foxhounds, with the vocabulary of both. In her domestic circle she comported herself in the arbitrary style that one attributes, probably without the least justification, to an American political Boss in the bosom of his caucus. The late Theodore Thropplestance had left her, some thirty-five years ago, in absolute possession of a considerable fortune, a large landed property, and a gallery full of valuable pictures. In those intervening years she had outlived her son and quarrelled with her elder grandson, who had married without her consent or approval. Bertie Thropplestance, her younger grandson, was the heir-designate to her property, and as such he was a centre of interest and concern to some half-hundred ambitious mothers with daughters of marriageable age. Bertie was an amiable, easy-going young man, who was quite ready to marry anyone who was favourably recommended to his notice, but he was not going to waste his time in falling in love with anyone who would come under his grandmother's veto. The favourable recommendation would have to come from Mrs. Thropplestance.

Teresa's house-parties were always rounded off

with a plentiful garnishing of presentable young women and alert, attendant mothers, but the old lady was emphatically discouraging whenever any one of her girl guests became at all likely to outbid the others as a possible granddaughter-in-law. It was the inheritance of her fortune and estate that was in question, and she was evidently disposed to exercise and enjoy her powers of selection and rejection to the utmost. Bertie's preferences did not greatly matter; he was of the sort who can be stolidly happy with any kind of wife; he had cheerfully put up with his grandmother all his life, so he was not likely to fret and fume over anything that might befall him in the way of a helpmate.

The party that gathered under Teresa's roof in Christmas week of the year nineteen-hundred-and-something was of smaller proportions than usual, and Mrs. Yonelet, who formed one of the party, was inclined to deduce hopeful augury from this circumstance. Dora Yonelet and Bertie were so obviously made for one another, she confided to the vicar's wife, and if the old lady were accustomed to seeing them about a lot together she might adopt the view that they would make a suitable married couple.

"People soon get used to an idea if it is dangled constantly before their eyes," said Mrs. Yonelet hopefully, "and the more often Teresa sees those young people together, happy in each other's company, the more she will get to take a kindly interest in Dora as a possible and desirable wife for Bertie."

"My dear," said the vicar's wife resignedly, "my own Sybil was thrown together with Bertie under the most romantic circumstances—I'll tell you about it some day—but it made no impression whatever on

Teresa; she put her foot down in the most uncompromising fashion, and Sybil married an Indian civilian."

"Quite right of her," said Mrs. Yonelet with vague approval; "it's what any girl of spirit would have done. Still, that was a year or two ago, I believe; Bertie is older now, and so is Teresa. Naturally she must be anxious to see him settled."

The vicar's wife reflected that Teresa seemed to be the one person who showed no immediate anxiety to supply Bertie with a wife, but she kept the thought to herself.

Mrs. Yonelet was a woman of resourceful energy and generalship; she involved the other members of the house-party, the deadweight, so to speak, in all manner of exercises and occupations that segregated them from Bertie and Dora, who were left to their own devisings—that is to say, to Dora's devisings and Bertie's accommodating acquiescence. Dora helped in the Christmas decorations of the parish church, and Bertie helped her to help. Together they fed the swans, till the birds went on a dyspepsia-strike, together they played billiards, together they photographed the village almshouses, and, at a respectful distance, the tame elk that browsed in solitary aloofness in the park. It was "tame" in the sense that it had long ago discarded the least vestige of fear of the human race; nothing in its record encouraged its human neighbours to feel a reciprocal confidence.

Whatever sport or exercise or occupation Bertie and Dora indulged in together was unfailingly chronicled and advertised by Mrs. Yonelet for the due enlightenment of Bertie's grandmother.

"Those two inseparables have just come in from

a bicycle ride," she would announce ; " quite a picture they make, so fresh and glowing after their spin."

" A picture needing words," would be Teresa's private comment, and as far as Bertie was concerned she was determined that the words should remain unspoken.

On the afternoon after Christmas Day Mrs. Yonelet dashed into the drawing-room, where her hostess was sitting amid a circle of guests and tea-cups and muffin-dishes. Fate had placed what seemed like a trump-card in the hands of the patiently-manœuvring mother. With eyes blazing with excitement and a voice heavily escorted with exclamation marks she made a dramatic announcement.

" Bertie has saved Dora from the elk ! "

In swift, excited sentences, broken with maternal emotion, she gave supplementary information as to how the treacherous animal had ambushed Dora as she was hunting for a strayed golf ball, and how Bertie had dashed to her rescue with a stable fork and driven the beast off in the nick of time.

" It was touch and go ! She threw her niblick at it, but that didn't stop it. In another moment she would have been crushed beneath its hoofs," panted Mrs. Yonelet.

" The animal is not safe," said Teresa, handing her agitated guest a cup of tea. " I forget if you take sugar. I suppose the solitary life it leads has soured its temper. There are muffins in the grate. It's not my fault ; I've tried to get it a mate for ever so long. You don't know of anyone with a lady elk for sale or exchange, do you ? " she asked the company generally.

But Mrs. Yonelet was in no humour to listen to

talk of elk marriages. The mating of two human beings was the subject uppermost in her mind, and the opportunity for advancing her pet project was too valuable to be neglected.

"Teresa," she exclaimed impressively, "after those two young people have been thrown together so dramatically, nothing can be quite the same again between them. Bertie has done more than save Dora's life; he has earned her affection. One cannot help feeling that Fate has consecrated them for one another."

"Exactly what the vicar's wife said when Bertie saved Sybil from the elk a year or two ago," observed Teresa placidly; "I pointed out to her that he had rescued Mirabel Hicks from the same predicament a few months previously, and that priority really belonged to the gardener's boy, who had been rescued in the January of that year. There is a good deal of sameness in country life, you know."

"It seems to be a very dangerous animal," said one of the guests.

"That's what the mother of the gardener's boy said," remarked Teresa; "she wanted me to have it destroyed, but I pointed out to her that she had eleven children and I had only one elk. I also gave her a black silk skirt; she said that though there hadn't been a funeral in her family, she felt as if there had been. Anyhow, we parted friends. I can't offer you a silk skirt, Emily, but you may have another cup of tea. As I have already remarked, there are muffins in the grate."

Teresa closed the discussion, having deftly conveyed the impression that she considered the mother of the gardener's boy had shown a far more reasonable spirit than the parents of other elk-assaulted victims.

"Teresa is devoid of feeling," said Mrs. Yonelet afterwards to the vicar's wife; "to sit there, talking of muffins, with an appalling tragedy only narrowly averted——"

"Of course you know whom she really intends Bertie to marry?" asked the vicar's wife; "I've noticed it for some time. The Bickelbys' German governess."

"A German governess! What an idea!" gasped Mrs. Yonelet.

"She's of quite good family, I believe," said the vicar's wife, "and not at all the mouse-in-the-background sort of person that governesses are usually supposed to be. In fact, next to Teresa, she's about the most assertive and combative personality in the neighbourhood. She's pointed out to my husband all sorts of errors in his sermons, and she gave Sir Laurence a public lecture on how he ought to handle the hounds. You know how sensitive Sir Laurence is about any criticism of his Mastership, and to have a governess laying down the law to him nearly drove him into a fit. She's behaved like that to every one, except, of course, Teresa, and every one has been defensively rude to her in return. The Bickelbys are simply too afraid of her to get rid of her. Now isn't that exactly the sort of woman whom Teresa would take a delight in installing as her successor? Imagine the discomfort and awkwardness in the county if we suddenly found that she was to be the future hostess at the Hall. Teresa's only regret will be that she won't be alive to see it."

"But," objected Mrs. Yonelet, "surely Bertie

hasn't shown the least sign of being attracted in that quarter?"

"Oh, she's quite nice-looking in a way, and dresses well, and plays a good game of tennis. She often comes across the park with messages from the Bickelby mansion, and one of these days Bertie will rescue her from the elk, which has become almost a habit with him, and Teresa will say that Fate has consecrated them to one another. Bertie might not be disposed to pay much attention to the consecrations of Fate, but he would not dream of opposing his grandmother."

The vicar's wife spoke with the quiet authority of one who has intuitive knowledge, and in her heart of hearts Mrs. Yonelet believed her.

Six months later the elk had to be destroyed. In a fit of exceptional moroseness it had killed the Bickelbys' German governess. It was an irony of its fate that it should achieve popularity in the last moments of its career; at any rate, it established the record of being the only living thing that had permanently thwarted Teresa Thropplestance's plans.

Dora Yonelet broke off her engagement with an Indian civilian, and married Bertie three months after his grandmother's death—Teresa did not long survive the German governess fiasco. At Christmas time every year young Mrs. Thropplestance hangs an extra large festoon of evergreens on the elk horns that decorate the hall.

"It was a fearsome beast," she observes to Bertie, "but I always feel that it was instrumental in bringing us together."

Which, of course, was true.

"DOWN PENS"

"HAVE you written to thank the Froplinsons for what they sent us?" asked Egbert.

"No," said Janetta, with a note of tired defiance in her voice; "I've written eleven letters to-day expressing surprise and gratitude for sundry unmerited gifts, but I haven't written to the Froplinsons."

"Some one will have to write to them," said Egbert.

"I don't dispute the necessity, but I don't think the some one should be me," said Janetta. "I wouldn't mind writing a letter of angry recrimination or heartless satire to some suitable recipient; in fact, I should rather enjoy it, but I've come to the end of my capacity for expressing servile amiability. Eleven letters to-day and nine yesterday, all couched in the same strain of ecstatic thankfulness: really, you can't expect me to sit down to another. There is such a thing as writing oneself out."

"I've written nearly as many," said Egbert, "and I've had my usual business correspondence to get through too. Besides, I don't know what it was that the Froplinsons sent us."

"A William the Conqueror calendar," said Janetta, "with a quotation of one of his great thoughts for every day in the year."

"Impossible," said Egbert; "he didn't have three hundred and sixty-five thoughts in the whole of his life, or, if he did, he kept them to himself. He was a man of action, not of introspection."

"Well, it was William Wordsworth, then," said Janetta; "I know William came into it somewhere."

"That sounds more probable," said Egbert; "well, let's collaborate on this letter of thanks and get it done. I'll dictate, and you can scribble it down. 'Dear Mrs. Froplinson—thank you and your husband so much for the very pretty calendar you sent us. It was very good of you to think of us.'"

"You can't possibly say that," said Janetta, laying down her pen.

"It's what I always do say, and what every one says to me," protested Egbert.

"We sent them something on the twenty-second," said Janetta, "so they simply *had* to think of us. There was no getting away from it."

"What did we send them?" asked Egbert gloomily.

"Bridge-markers," said Janetta, "in a cardboard case, with some inanity about 'digging for fortune with a royal spade' emblazoned on the cover. The moment I saw it in the shop I said to myself 'Froplinsons' and to the attendant 'How much?' When he said 'Ninepence,' I gave him their address, jabbed our card in, paid tenpence or elevenpence to cover the postage, and thanked heaven. With less sincerity and infinitely more trouble they eventually thanked me."

"The Froplinsons don't play bridge," said Egbert.

"One is not supposed to notice social deformities of that sort," said Janetta; "it wouldn't be polite. Besides, what trouble did they take to find out whether we read Wordsworth with gladness? For all they knew or cared we might be frantically embedded in he belief that all poetry begins and ends with John Masefield, and it might infuriate or depress us to have a daily sample of Wordsworthian products flung at us."

"Well, let's get on with the letter of thanks," said Egbert.

"Proceed," said Janetta.

"'How clever of you to guess that Wordsworth is our favourite poet,'" dictated Egbert.

Again Janetta laid down her pen.

"Do you realize what that means?" she asked; "a Wordsworth booklet next Christmas, and another calendar the Christmas after, with the same problem of having to write suitable letters of thankfulness. No, the best thing to do is to drop all further allusion to the calendar and switch off on to some other topic."

"But what other topic?"

"Oh, something like this: 'What do you think of the New Year Honours List? A friend of ours made such a clever remark when he read it.' Then you can stick in any remark that comes into your head; it needn't be clever. The Froplinsons won't know whether it is or isn't."

"We don't even know on which side they are in politics," objected Egbert; "and anyhow you can't suddenly dismiss the subject of the calendar. Surely there must be some intelligent remark that can be made about it."

"Well, we can't think of one," said Janetta wearily; "the fact is, we've both written ourselves out. Heavens! I've just remembered Mrs. Stephen Ludberry. I haven't thanked her for what she sent."

"What did she send?"

"I forget; I think it was a calendar."

There was a long silence, the forlorn silence of those who are bereft of hope and have almost ceased to care.

Presently Egbert started from his seat with an air of resolution. The light of battle was in his eyes.

"Let me come to the writing-table," he exclaimed.

"Gladly," said Janetta. "Are you going to write to Mrs. Ludberry or the Froplinsons?"

"To neither," said Egbert, drawing a stack of note-paper towards him; "I'm going to write to the editor of every enlightened and influential newspaper in the Kingdom. I'm going to suggest that there should be a sort of epistolary Truce of God during the festivities of Christmas and New Year. From the twenty-fourth of December to the third or fourth of January it shall be considered an offence against good sense and good feeling to write or expect any letter or communication that does not deal with the necessary events of the moment. Answers to invitations, arrangements about trains, renewal of club subscriptions, and, of course, all the ordinary everyday affairs of business, sickness, engaging new cooks, and so forth, these will be dealt with in the usual manner as something inevitable, a legitimate part of our daily life. But all the devastating accretions of correspondence, incident to the festive season, these should be swept away to give the season a chance of being really festive, a time of untroubled, unpunctuated peace and good will."

"But you would have to make some acknowledgment of presents received," objected Janetta; "otherwise people would never know whether they had arrived safely."

"Of course, I have thought of that," said Egbert; "every present that was sent off would be accompanied by a ticket bearing the date of dispatch and the signature of the sender, and some conventional hieroglyphic to show that it was intended to be a Christmas or New Year gift; there would be a counterfoil with space for the recipient's name and the date of arrival, and all you would have to do would be to sign and date the counterfoil, add a conventional hieroglyphic indicating heartfelt thanks and gratified surprise, put the thing into an envelope and post it."

"It sounds delightfully simple," said Janetta wistfully, "but people would consider it too cut-and-dried, too perfunctory."

"It is not a bit more perfunctory than the present system," said Egbert; "I have only the same conventional language of gratitude at my disposal with which to thank dear old Colonel Chuttle for his perfectly delicious Stilton, which we shall devour to the last morsel, and the Froplinsons for their calendar, which we shall never look at. Colonel Chuttle knows that we are grateful for the Stilton, without having to be told so, and the Froplinsons know that we are bored with their calendar, whatever we may say to the contrary, just as we know that they are bored with the bridge-markers in spite of their written assurance that they thanked us for our charming little gift. What is more, the Colonel knows that even if we had taken a sudden aversion to Stilton or been forbidden it by the doctor, we should still have written a letter of hearty thanks around it. So you see the present system of acknowledgment is just as perfunctory and conventional as the counterfoil business would be, only ten times more tiresome and brain-racking."

"Your plan would certainly bring the ideal of a Happy Christmas a step nearer realization," said Janetta.

"There are exceptions, of course," said Egbert, "people who really try to infuse a breath of reality into their letters of acknowledgment. Aunt Susan, for instance, who writes: 'Thank you very much for the ham; not such a good flavour as the one you sent last year, which itself was not a particularly good one. Hams are not what they used to be.' It would be a pity to be deprived of her Christmas comments, but that loss would be swallowed up in the general gain."

"Meanwhile," said Janetta, "what *am* I to say to the Froplinsons?"

THE NAME-DAY

ADVENTURES, according to the proverb, are to the adventurous. Quite as often they are to the non-adventurous, to the retiring, to the constitutionally timid. John James Abbleway had been endowed by Nature with the sort of disposition that instinctively avoids Carlist intrigues, slum crusades, the tracking of wounded wild beasts, and the moving of hostile amendments at political meetings. If a mad dog or a Mad Mullah had come his way he would have surrendered the way without hesitation. At school he had unwillingly acquired a thorough knowledge of the German tongue out of deference to the plainly-expressed wishes of a foreign-languages master, who, though he taught modern subjects, employed old-fashioned methods in driving his lessons home. It was this enforced familiarity with an important commercial language which thrust Abbleway in later years into strange lands where adventures were less easy to guard against than in the ordered atmosphere of an English country town. The firm that he worked for saw fit to send him one day on a prosaic business errand to the far city of Vienna, and, having sent him there, continued to keep him there, still engaged in humdrum affairs of commerce, but with the possibilities of romance and adventure, or even misadventure, jostling at his elbow. After two and a half years of exile, however, John James Abbleway had embarked on only one hazardous undertaking, and that was of a nature which would assuredly have overtaken him sooner or later if he had been leading a sheltered, stay-at-home existence at Dorking or Huntingdon. He fell placidly in love with a placidly lovable English girl, the sister of one of his commercial colleagues, who was improving her mind by a short trip to foreign parts, and in due course he was formally accepted as the young man she was engaged to. The further step by which she was to become Mrs. John Abbleway was to take place a twelvemonth hence in a town in the English midlands, by which time the firm that employed John James would have no further need for his presence in the Austrian capital.

It was early in April, two months after the installation of Abbleway as the young man Miss Penning was engaged to, when he received a letter from her, written from Venice. She was still peregrinating under the wing of her brother, and as the latter's business arrangements would take him across to Fiume for a day or two, she had conceived the idea that it would be rather jolly if John could obtain leave of absence and run down to the Adriatic coast to meet them. She had looked up the route on the map, and the journey did not appear likely to be expensive. Between the lines of her communication there lay a hint that if he really cared for her——

Abbleway obtained leave of absence and added a journey to Fiume to his life's adventures. He left Vienna on a cold, cheerless day. The flower shops were full of spring blooms, and the weekly organs of illustrated humour were full of spring topics, but the skies were heavy with clouds that looked like cotton-wool that has been kept over long in a shop window.

"Snow comes," said the train official to the station officials; and they agreed that snow was about to come. And it came, rapidly, plenteously. The train had not been more than an hour on its journey when the cotton-wool clouds commenced to dissolve in a blinding downpour of snowflakes. The forest trees on either side of the line were speedily coated with a heavy white mantle, the telegraph wires became thick glistening ropes, the line itself was buried more and more completely under a carpeting of snow, through which the not very powerful engine ploughed its way with increasing difficulty. The Vienna-Fiume line is scarcely the best equipped of the Austrian State railways, and Abbleway began to have serious fears for a breakdown. The train had slowed down to a painful and precarious crawl and presently came to a halt at a spot where the drifting snow had accumulated in a formidable barrier. The engine made a special effort and broke through the obstruction, but in the course of another twenty minutes it was again held up. The process of breaking through was renewed and the train doggedly resumed its way, encountering and surmounting fresh hindrances at frequent intervals. After a standstill of unusually long duration in a particularly deep drift the compartment in which Abbleway was sitting gave a huge jerk and a lurch, and then seemed to remain stationary; it undoubtedly was not moving, and yet he could hear the puffing of the engine and the slow rumbling and jolting of wheels. The puffing and rumbling grew fainter, as though it were dying away through the agency of intervening distance. Abbleway suddenly gave vent to an exclamation of scandalized alarm, opened the window, and peered out into the snowstorm. The flakes perched on his eyelashes and blurred his vision, but he saw enough t[o] help him to realize what had happened. The engin[e] had made a mighty plunge through the drift and ha[d] gone merrily forward, lightened of the load of its rea[r] carriage, whose coupling had snapped under the strain. Abbleway was alone, or almost alone, with a derelic[t] railway waggon, in the heart of some Styrian o[r] Croatian forest. In the third-class compartment nex[t] to his own he remembered to have seen a peasant woman, who had entered the train at a small wayside station. "With the exception of that woman," he exclaimed dramatically to himself, "the nearest living beings are probably a pack of wolves."

Before making his way to the third-class compartment to acquaint his fellow-traveller with the extent of the disaster Abbleway hurriedly pondered the question of the woman's nationality. He had acquired a smattering of Slavonic tongues during his residence in Vienna, and felt competent to grapple with several racial possibilities.

"If she is Croat or Serb or Bosniak I shall be able to make her understand," he promised himself. "If she is Magyar, heaven help me! We shall have to converse entirely by signs."

He entered the carriage and made his momentous announcement in the best approach to Croat speech that he could achieve.

"The train has broken away and left us!"

The woman shook her head with a movement that might be intended to convey resignation to the will of heaven, but probably meant noncomprehension. Abbleway repeated his information with variations of Slavonic tongues and generous displays of pantomime.

"Ah," said the woman at last in German dialect, "the train has gone? We are left. Ah, so."

She seemed about as much interested as though Abbleway had told her the result of the municipal elections in Amsterdam.

"They will find out at some station, and when the line is clear of snow they will send an engine. It happens that way sometimes."

"We may be here all night!" exclaimed Abbleway.

The woman looked as though she thought it possible.

"Are there wolves in these parts?" asked Abbleway hurriedly.

"Many," said the woman; "just outside this forest my aunt was devoured three years ago, as she was coming home from market. The horse and a young pig that was in the cart were eaten too. The horse was a very old one, but it was a beautiful young pig, oh, so fat. I cried when I heard that it was taken. They spare nothing."

"They may attack us here," said Abbleway tremulously; "they could easily break in, these carriages are like matchwood. We may both be devoured."

"You, perhaps," said the woman calmly; "not me."

"Why not you?" demanded Abbleway.

"It is the day of Saint Mariä Kleophä, my name-day. She would not allow me to be eaten by wolves on her day. Such a thing could not be thought of. You, yes, but not me."

Abbleway changed the subject.

"It is only afternoon now; if we are to be left here till morning we shall be starving."

"I have here some good eatables," said the woman

tranquilly; "on my festival day it is natural that I should have provision with me. I have five good blood-sausages; in the town shops they cost twenty-five heller each. Things are dear in the town shops."

"I will give you fifty heller apiece for a couple of them," said Abbleway with some enthusiasm.

"In a railway accident things become very dear," said the woman; "these blood-sausages are four kronen apiece."

"Four kronen!" exclaimed Abbleway; "four kronen for a blood sausage!"

"You cannot get them any cheaper on this train," said the woman, with relentless logic, "because there aren't any others to get. In Agram you can buy them cheaper, and in Paradise no doubt they will be given to us for nothing, but here they cost four kronen each. I have a small piece of Emmenthaler cheese and a honey-cake and a piece of bread that I can let you have. That will be another three kronen, eleven kronen in all. There is a piece of ham, but that I cannot let you have on my name-day."

Abbleway wondered to himself what price she would have put on the ham, and hurried to pay her the eleven kronen before her emergency tariff expanded into a famine tariff. As he was taking possession of his modest store of eatables he suddenly heard a noise which set his heart thumping in a miserable fever of fear. There was a scraping and shuffling as of some animal or animals trying to climb up to the footboard. In another moment, through the snow-encrusted glass of the carriage window, he saw a gaunt prick-eared head, with gaping jaw and lolling tongue and gleaming teeth; a second later another head shot up.

"There are hundreds of them," whispered Ableway; "they have scented us. They will tear the carriage to pieces. We shall be devoured."

"Not me, on my name-day. The holy Mariä Kleophä would not permit it," said the woman with provoking calm.

The heads dropped down from the window and an uncanny silence fell on the beleaguered carriage. Abbleway neither moved nor spoke. Perhaps the brutes had not clearly seen or winded the human occupants of the carriage, and had prowled away on some other errand of rapine.

The long torture-laden minutes passed slowly away.

"It grows cold," said the woman suddenly, crossing over to the far end of the carriage, where the heads had appeared. "The heating apparatus does not work any longer. See, over there beyond the trees, there is a chimney with smoke coming from it. It is not far, and the snow has nearly stopped. I shall find a path through the forest to that house with the chimney."

"But the wolves!" exclaimed Abbleway; "they may——"

"Not on my name-day," said the woman obstinately, and before he could stop her she had opened the door and climbed down into the snow. A moment later he hid his face in his hands; two gaunt lean figures rushed upon her from the forest. No doubt she had courted her fate, but Abbleway had no wish to see a human being torn to pieces and devoured before his eyes.

When he looked at last a new sensation of scandalized astonishment took possession of him. He had been straitly brought up in a small English town, and he was not prepared to be the witness of a miracle. The wolves were not doing anything worse to the woman than drench her with snow as they gambolled round her.

A short, joyous bark revealed the clue to the situation.

"Are those—dogs?" he called weakly.

"My cousin Karl's dogs, yes," she answered; "that is his inn, over beyond the trees. I knew it was there, but I did not want to take you there; he is always grasping with strangers. However, it grows too cold to remain in the train. Ah, ah, see what comes!"

A whistle sounded, and a relief engine made its appearance, snorting its way sulkily through the snow. Abbleway did not have the opportunity for finding out whether Karl was really avaricious.

THE LUMBER-ROOM

THE children were to be driven, as a special treat, to the sands at Jagborough. Nicholas was not to be of the party; he was in disgrace. Only that morning he had refused to eat his wholesome bread-and-milk on the seemingly frivolous ground that there was a frog in it. Older and wiser and better people had told him that there could not possibly be a frog in his bread-and-milk and that he was not to talk nonsense; he continued, nevertheless, to talk what seemed the veriest nonsense, and described with much detail the colouration and markings of the alleged frog. The dramatic part of the incident was that there really was a frog in Nicholas' basin of bread-and-milk; he had put it there himself, so he felt entitled to know something about it. The sin of taking a frog from the garden and putting it into a bowl of wholesome bread-and-milk was enlarged on at great length, but the fact that stood out clearest in the whole affair, as it presented itself to the mind of Nicholas, was that the older, wiser, and better people had been proved to be profoundly in error in matters about which they had expressed the utmost assurance.

"You said there couldn't possibly be a frog in my bread-and-milk; there *was* a frog in my bread-and-milk," he repeated, with the insistence of a skilled tactician who does not intend to shift from favourable ground.

So his boy-cousin and girl-cousin and his quit
uninteresting younger brother were to be taken t
Jagborough sands that afternoon and he was to sta
at home. His cousins' aunt, who insisted, by a
unwarranted stretch of imagination, in styling hersel
his aunt also, had hastily invented the Jagboroug
expedition in order to impress on Nicholas the delight
that he had justly forfeited by his disgraceful conduc
at the breakfast-table. It was her habit, whenever
one of the children fell from grace, to improvise
something of a festival nature from which the offender
would be rigorously debarred ; if all the children
sinned collectively they were suddenly informed of a
circus in a neighbouring town, a circus of unrivalled
merit and uncounted elephants, to which, but for their
depravity, they would have been taken that very day.

A few decent tears were looked for on the part of Nicholas when the moment for the departure of the expedition arrived. As a matter of fact, however, all the crying was done by his girl-cousin, who scraped her knee rather painfully against the step of the carriage as she was scrambling in.

"How she did howl," said Nicholas cheerfully, as the party drove off without any of the elation of high spirits that should have characterized it.

"She'll soon get over that," said the *soi-disant* aunt ; "it will be a glorious afternoon for racing about over those beautiful sands. How they will enjoy themselves !"

"Bobby won't enjoy himself much, and he won't race much either," said Nicholas with a grim chuckle ; "his boots are hurting him. They're too tight."

"Why didn't he tell me they were hurting ?" asked the aunt with some asperity.

"He told you twice, but you weren't listening. You often don't listen when we tell you important things."

"You are not to go into the gooseberry garden," said the aunt, changing the subject.

"Why not?" demanded Nicholas.

"Because you are in disgrace," said the aunt loftily.

Nicholas did not admit the flawlessness of the reasoning; he felt perfectly capable of being in disgrace and in a gooseberry garden at the same moment. His face took on an expression of considerable obstinacy. It was clear to his aunt that he was determined to get into the gooseberry garden, "only," as she remarked to herself, "because I have told him he is not to."

Now the gooseberry garden had two doors by which it might be entered, and once a small person like Nicholas could slip in there he could effectually disappear from view amid the masking growth of artichokes, raspberry canes, and fruit bushes. The aunt had many other things to do that afternoon, but she spent an hour or two in trivial gardening operations among flower beds and shrubberies, whence she could keep a watchful eye on the two doors that led to the forbidden paradise. She was a woman of few ideas, with immense powers of concentration.

Nicholas made one or two sorties into the front garden, wriggling his way with obvious stealth of purpose towards one or other of the doors, but never able for a moment to evade the aunt's watchful eye. As a matter of fact, he had no intention of trying to get into the gooseberry garden, but it was extremely convenient for him that his aunt should believe that he had; it was a belief that would keep her on self-imposed sentry-duty for the greater part of the afternoon. Having thoroughly confirmed and fortified her suspicions, Nicholas slipped back into the house and rapidly put into execution a plan of action that had long germinated in his brain. By standing on a chair in the library one could reach a shelf on which reposed a fat, important-looking key. The key was as important as it looked; it was the instrument which kept the mysteries of the lumber-room secure from unauthorized intrusion, which opened a way only for aunts and such-like privileged persons. Nicholas had not had much experience of the art of fitting keys into keyholes and turning locks, but for some days past he had practised with the key of the schoolroom door; he did not believe in trusting too much to luck and accident. The key turned stiffly in the lock, but it turned. The door opened, and Nicholas was in an unknown land, compared with which the gooseberry garden was a stale delight, a mere material pleasure.

Often and often Nicholas had pictured to himself what the lumber-room might be like, that region that was so carefully sealed from youthful eyes and concerning which no questions were ever answered. It came up to his expectations. In the first place it was large and dimly lit, one high window opening on to the forbidden garden being its only source of illumination. In the second place it was a storehouse of unimagined treasures. The aunt-by-assertion was one of those people who think that things spoil by use and consign them to dust and damp by way of preserving them. Such parts of the house as Nicholas knew best were rather bare and cheerless, but here there were wonderful things for the eye to feast on. First and foremost there was a piece of framed tapestry that was evidently meant to be a fire-screen. To Nicholas it was a living, breathing story; he sat down on a roll of Indian hangings, glowing in wonderful colours beneath a layer of dust, and took in all the details of the tapestry picture. A man, dressed in the hunting costume of some remote period, had just transfixed a stag with an arrow; it could not have been a difficult shot because the stag was only one or two paces away from him; in the thickly-growing vegetation that the picture suggested it would not have been difficult to creep up to a feeding stag, and the two spotted dogs that were springing forward to join in the chase had evidently been trained to keep to heel till the arrow was discharged. That part of the picture was simple, if interesting, but did the huntsman see, what Nicholas saw, that four galloping wolves were coming in his direction through the wood? There might be more than four of them hidden behind the trees, and in any case would the man and his dogs be able to cope with the four wolves if they made an attack? The man had only two arrows left in his quiver, and he might miss with one or both of them; all one knew about his skill in shooting was that he could hit a large stag at a ridiculously short range. Nicholas sat for many golden minutes revolving the possibilities of the scene; he was inclined to think that there were more than four wolves and that the man and his dogs were in a tight corner.

But there were other objects of delight and interest claiming his instant attention: there were quaint twisted candlesticks in the shape of snakes, and a teapot fashioned like a china duck, out of whose open beak the tea was supposed to come. How dull and shapeless the nursery teapot seemed in comparison! And there was a carved sandal-wood box packed tight with aromatic cottonwool, and between the layers of cottonwool were little brass figures, hump-necked bulls, and peacocks and goblins, delightful to see and to handle. Less promising in appearance was a large square book with plain black covers; Nicholas peeped into it, and, behold, it was full of coloured pictures of birds. And such birds! In the garden, and in the lanes when he went for a walk, Nicholas came across a few birds, of which the largest were an occasional magpie or wood-pigeon; here were herons and bustards, kites, toucans, tiger-bitterns, brush turkeys, ibises, golden pheasants, a whole portrait gallery of undreamed-of creatures. And as he was admiring the colouring of the mandarin duck and assigning a life-history to it, the voice of his aunt in shrill vociferation of his name came from the gooseberry garden without. She had grown suspicious at his long disappearance, and had leapt to the conclusion that he had climbed over the wall behind the sheltering screen of the lilac bushes; she was now engaged in energetic and rather hopeless search for him among the artichokes and raspberry canes.

"Nicholas, Nicholas!" she screamed, "you are to come out of this at once. It's no use trying to hide there; I can see you all the time."

It was probably the first time for twenty years that anyone had smiled in that lumber-room.

Presently the angry repetitions of Nicholas' name gave way to a shriek, and a cry for somebody to come quickly. Nicholas shut the book, restored it carefully to its place in a corner, and shook some dust from a neighbouring pile of newspapers over it. Then he crept from the room, locked the door, and replaced the key exactly where he had found it. His aunt was still calling his name when he sauntered into the front garden.

"Who's calling?" he asked.

"Me," came the answer from the other side of the wall; "didn't you hear me? I've been looking for you in the gooseberry garden, and I've slipped into the rain-water tank. Luckily there's no water in it, but the sides are slippery and I can't get out. Fetch the little ladder from under the cherry tree——"

"I was told I wasn't to go into the gooseberry garden," said Nicholas promptly.

"I told you not to, and now I tell you that you may," came the voice from the rain-water tank, rather impatiently.

"Your voice doesn't sound like aunt's," objected Nicholas; "you may be the Evil One tempting me to be disobedient. Aunt often tells me that the Evil One tempts me and that I always yield. This time I'm not going to yield."

"Don't talk nonsense," said the prisoner in the tank; "go and fetch the ladder."

"Will there be strawberry jam for tea?" asked Nicholas innocently.

"Certainly there will be," said the aunt, privately resolving that Nicholas should have none of it.

"Now I know that you are the Evil One and not aunt," shouted Nicholas gleefully; "when we asked aunt for strawberry jam yesterday she said there wasn't any. I know there are four jars of it in the store cupboard, because I looked, and of course you know it's there, but *she* doesn't, because she said there wasn't any. Oh, Devil, you *have* sold yourself!"

There was an unusual sense of luxury in being able to talk to an aunt as though one was talking to the Evil One, but Nicholas knew, with childish discernment, that such luxuries were not to be over-indulged in. He walked noisily away, and it was a kitchenmaid, in search of parsley, who eventually rescued the aunt from the rain-water tank.

Tea that evening was partaken of in a fearsome silence. The tide had been at its highest when the children had arrived at Jagborough Cove, so there had been no sands to play on—a circumstance that the aunt had overlooked in the haste of organizing her punitive expedition. The tightness of Bobby's boots had had disastrous effect on his temper the whole of the afternoon, and altogether the children could not have been said to have enjoyed themselves. The aunt maintained the frozen muteness of one who has suffered undignified and unmerited detention in a rain-water tank for thirty-five minutes. As for Nicholas, he, too, was silent, in the absorption of one who has much to think about; it was just possible, he considered, that the huntsman would escape with his hounds while the wolves feasted on the stricken stag.

FUR

"YOU look worried, dear," said Eleanor.

"I am worried," admitted Suzanne; "not worried exactly, but anxious. You see, my birthday happens next week——"

"You lucky person," interrupted Eleanor; "my birthday doesn't come till the end of March."

"Well, old Bertram Kneyght is over in England just now from the Argentine. He's a kind of distant cousin of my mother's, and so enormously rich that we've never let the relationship drop out of sight. Even if we don't see him or hear from him for years he is always Cousin Bertram when he does turn up. I can't say he's ever been of much solid use to us, but yesterday the subject of my birthday cropped up, and he asked me to let him know what I wanted for a present."

"Now I understand the anxiety," observed Eleanor.

"As a rule when one is confronted with a problem like that," said Suzanne, "all one's ideas vanish; one doesn't seem to have a desire in the world. Now it so happens that I have been very keen on a little Dresden figure that I saw somewhere in Kensington; about thirty-six shillings, quite beyond my means. I was very nearly describing the figure, and giving Bertram the address of the shop. And then it suddenly struck me that thirty-six shillings was such a ridiculously inadequate sum for a man of his immense wealth to spend on a birthday present. He could give thirty-six pounds as easily as you or I could buy a bunch of violets. I don't want to be greedy, of course, but I don't like being wasteful."

"The question is," said Eleanor, "what are his ideas as to present-giving? Some of the wealthiest people have curiously cramped views on that subject. When people grow gradually rich their requirements and standard of living expand in proportion, while their present-giving instincts often remain in the undeveloped condition of their earlier days. Something showy and not-too-expensive in a shop is their only conception of the ideal gift. That is why even quite good shops have their counters and windows crowded with things worth about four shillings that look as if they might be worth seven-and-six, and are priced at ten shillings and labelled 'seasonable gifts.'"

"I know," said Suzanne; "that is why it is so risky to be vague when one is giving indications of one's wants. Now if I say to him: 'I am going out to Davos this winter, so anything in the travelling line would be acceptable,' he *might* give me a dressing-bag with gold-mounted fittings, but, on the other hand, he might give me Baedeker's Switzerland, or 'Ski-ing without Tears,' or something of that sort."

"He would be more likely to say: 'She'll be going to lots of dances, a fan will be sure to be useful.'"

"Yes, and I've got tons of fans, so you see where the danger and anxiety lies. Now if there is one thing more than another that I really urgently want it is furs. I simply haven't any. I'm told that Davos is full of Russians, and they are sure to wear the most lovely sables and things. To be among people who are smothered in furs when one hasn't any oneself makes one want to break most of the Commandments."

"If it's furs that you're out for," said Eleanor, "you will have to superintend the choice of them in person. You can't be sure that your cousin knows the difference between silver-fox and ordinary squirrel."

"There are some heavenly silver-fox stoles at Goliath and Mastodon's," said Suzanne, with a sigh; "if I could only inveigle Bertram into their building and take him for a stroll through the fur department!"

"He lives somewhere near there, doesn't he?" said Eleanor. "Do you know what his habits are? Does he take a walk at any particular time of day?"

"He usually walks down to his club about three o'clock, if it's a fine day. That takes him right past Goliath and Mastodon's."

"Let us two meet him accidentally at the street corner to-morrow," said Eleanor; "we can walk a little way with him, and with luck we ought to be able to side-track him into the shop. You can say you want to get a hair-net or something. When we're safely there I can say: 'I wish you'd tell me what you want for your birthday.' Then you'll have everything ready to hand—the rich cousin, the fur department, and the topic of birthday presents."

"It's a great idea," said Suzanne; "you really are a brick. Come round to-morrow at twenty to three; don't be late, we must carry out our ambush to the minute."

At a few minutes to three the next afternoon the fur-trappers walked warily towards the selected corner. In the near distance rose the colossal pile of Messrs. Goliath and Mastodon's famed establishment. The afternoon was brilliantly fine, exactly the sort of weather to tempt a gentleman of advancing years into the discreet exercise of a leisurely walk.

"I say, dear, I wish you'd do something for me this evening," said Eleanor to her companion; "just drop in after dinner on some pretext or other, and stay on to make a fourth at bridge with Adela and the aunts. Otherwise I shall have to play, and Harry Scarisbrooke is going to come in unexpectedly about nine-fifteen, and I particularly wanted to be free to talk to him while the others are playing."

"Sorry, my dear, no can do," said Suzanne; "ordinary bridge at threepence a hundred, with such dreadfully slow players as your aunts, bores me to tears. I nearly go to sleep over it."

"But I most particularly want an opportunity to talk with Harry," urged Eleanor, an angry glint coming into her eyes.

"Sorry, anything to oblige, but not that," said Suzanne cheerfully; the sacrifices of friendship were beautiful in her eyes as long as she was not asked to make them.

Eleanor said nothing further on the subject, but the corners of her mouth rearranged themselves.

"There's our man!" exclaimed Suzanne suddenly; "hurry!"

Mr. Bertram Kneyght greeted his cousin and her friend with genuine heartiness, and readily accepted their invitation to explore the crowded mart that stood temptingly at their elbow. The plate-glass doors swung open and the trio plunged bravely into the jostling throng of buyers and loiterers.

"Is it always as full as this?" asked Bertram of Eleanor.

"More or less, and autumn sales are on just now," she replied.

Suzanne, in her anxiety to pilot her cousin to the desired haven of the fur department, was usually a few paces ahead of the others, coming back to them now and then if they lingered for a moment at some attractive counter, with the nervous solicitude of a parent rook encouraging its young ones on their first flying expedition.

"It's Suzanne's birthday on Wednesday next," confided Eleanor to Bertram Kneyght at a moment when Suzanne had left them unusually far behind; "my birthday comes the day before, so we are both on the look-out for something to give each other."

"Ah," said Bertram. "Now, perhaps you can advise me on that very point. I want to give Suzanne something, and I haven't the least idea what she wants."

"She's rather a problem," said Eleanor. "She seems to have everything one can think of, lucky girl. A fan is always useful; she'll be going to a lot of dances at Davos this winter. Yes, I should think a fan would please her more than anything. After our birthdays are over we inspect each other's muster of presents, and I always feel dreadfully humble. She gets such nice things, and I never have anything worth showing. You see, none of my relations or any of the people who give me presents are at all well off, so I can't expect them to do anything more than just remember the day with some little trifle. Two years ago an uncle on my mother's side of the family, who had come into a small legacy, promised me a silver-fox stole for my birthday. I can't tell you how excited I was about it, how I pictured myself showing it off to all my friends and enemies. Then just at that moment his wife died, and, of course, poor man, he could not be expected to think of birthday presents at such a time. He has lived abroad ever since, and I never got my fur. Do you know, to this day I can scarcely look at a silver-fox pelt in a shop window or round anyone's neck without feeling ready to burst into tears. I suppose if I hadn't had the prospect of getting one I shouldn't feel that way. Look, there is the fan counter, on your left; you can easily slip away in the crowd. Get her as nice a one as you can see—she is such a dear, dear girl."

"Hullo, I thought I had lost you," said Suzanne, making her way through an obstructive knot of shoppers. "Where is Bertram?"

"I got separated from him long ago. I thought he was on ahead with you," said Eleanor. "We shall never find him in this crush."

Which turned out to be a true prediction.

"All our trouble and forethought thrown away," said Suzanne sulkily, when they had pushed their way fruitlessly through half a dozen departments.

"I can't think why you didn't grab him by the arm," said Eleanor; "I would have if I'd known him longer, but I'd only just been introduced. It's nearly four now, we'd better have tea."

Some days later Suzanne rang Eleanor up on the telephone.

"Thank you very much for the photograph frame. It was just what I wanted. Very good of you. I say, do you know what that Kneyght person has given me? Just what you said he would—a wretched fan. What? Oh yes, quite a good enough fan in its way, but still. . . ."

"You must come and see what he's given me," came in Eleanor's voice over the 'phone.

"You! Why should he give you anything?"

"Your cousin appears to be one of those rare people of wealth who take a pleasure in giving good presents," came the reply.

"I wondered why he was so anxious to know where she lived," snapped Suzanne to herself as she rang off.

A cloud has arisen between the friendships of the two young women; as far as Eleanor is concerned the cloud has a silver-fox lining.

THE PHILANTHROPIST AND THE HAPPY CAT

JOCANTHA BESSBURY was in the mood to be serenely and graciously happy. Her world was a pleasant place, and it was wearing one of its pleasantest aspects. Gregory had managed to get home for a hurried lunch and a smoke afterwards in the little snuggery; the lunch had been a good one, and there was just time to do justice to the coffee and cigarettes. Both were excellent in their way, and Gregory was, in this way, an excellent husband. Jocantha rather suspected herself of making him a very charming wife, and more than suspected herself of having a first-rate dressmaker.

"I don't suppose a more thoroughly contented personality is to be found in all Chelsea," observed Jocantha in allusion to herself; "except perhaps Attab," she continued, glancing towards the large tabby-marked cat that lay in considerable ease in a corner of the divan. "He lies there, purring and dreaming, shifting his limbs now and then in an ecstasy of cushioned comfort. He seems the incarnation of everything soft and silky and velvety, without a sharp edge in his composition, a dreamer whose philosophy is sleep and let sleep; and then, as evening draws on, he goes out into the garden with a red glint in his eyes and slays a drowsy sparrow."

"As every pair of sparrows hatches out ten or

more young ones in the year, while their food supply remains stationary, it is just as well that the Attabs of the community should have that idea of how to pass an amusing afternoon," said Gregory. Having delivered himself of this sage comment he lit another cigarette, bade Jocantha a playfully affectionate good-bye, and departed into the outer world.

"Remember, dinner's a wee bit earlier to-night, as we're going to the Haymarket," she called after him.

Left to herself, Jocantha continued the process of looking at her life with placid, introspective eyes. If she had not everything she wanted in this world, at least she was very well pleased with what she had got. She was very well pleased, for instance, with the snuggery, which contrived somehow to be cosy and dainty and expensive all at once. The porcelain was rare and beautiful, the Chinese enamels took on wonderful tints in the firelight, the rugs and hangings led the eye through sumptuous harmonies of colouring. It was a room in which one might have suitably entertained an ambassador or an archbishop, but it was also a room in which one could cut out pictures for a scrap-book without feeling that one was scandalizing the deities of the place with one's litter. And as with the snuggery, so with the rest of the house, and as with the house, so with the other departments of Jocantha's life; she really had good reason for being one of the most contented women in Chelsea.

From being in a mood of simmering satisfaction with her lot she passed to the phase of being generously commiserating for those thousands around her whose lives and circumstances were dull, cheap, pleasureless, and empty. Work girls, shop assistants and so forth, the class that have neither the happy-go-lucky freedom of the poor nor the leisured freedom of the rich, came specially within the range of her sympathy. It was sad to think that there were young people who, after a long day's work, had to sit alone in chill, dreary bedrooms because they could not afford the price of a cup of coffee and a sandwich in a restaurant, still less a shilling for a theatre gallery.

Jocantha's mind was still dwelling on this theme when she started forth on an afternoon campaign of desultory shopping; it would be rather a comforting thing, she told herself, if she could do something, on the spur of the moment, to bring a gleam of pleasure and interest into the life of even one or two wistful-hearted, empty-pocketed workers; it would add a good deal to her sense of enjoyment at the theatre that night. She would get two upper circle tickets for a popular play, make her way into some cheap tea-shop, and present the tickets to the first couple of interesting work girls with whom she could casually drop into conversation. She could explain matters by saying that she was unable to use the tickets herself and did not want them to be wasted, and, on the other hand, did not want the trouble of sending them back. On further reflection she decided that it might be better to get only one ticket and give it to some lonely-looking girl sitting eating her frugal meal by herself; the girl might scrape acquaintance with her next-seat neighbour at the theatre and lay the foundations of a lasting friendship.

With the Fairy Godmother impulse strong upon her, Jocantha marched into a ticket agency and selected with immense care an upper circle seat for the "Yellow Peacock," a play that was attracting a considerable amount of discussion and criticism. Then she went forth in search of a tea-shop and philanthropic adventure, at about the same time that Attab sauntered into the garden with a mind attuned to sparrow stalking. In a corner of an A.B.C. shop she found an unoccupied table, whereat she promptly installed herself, impelled by the fact that at the next table was sitting a young girl, rather plain of feature, with tired, listless eyes and a general air of uncomplaining forlornness. Her dress was of poor material, but aimed at being in the fashion, her hair was pretty, and her complexion bad; she was finishing a modest meal of tea and scone, and she was not very different in her way from thousands of other girls who were finishing, or beginning, or continuing their teas in London tea-shops at that exact moment. The odds were enormously in favour of the supposition that she had never seen the "Yellow Peacock"; obviously she supplied excellent material for Jocantha's first experiment in haphazard benefaction.

Jocantha ordered some tea and a muffin, and then turned a friendly scrutiny on her neighbour with a view to catching her eye. At that precise moment the girl's face lit up with sudden pleasure, her eyes sparkled, a flush came into her cheeks, and she looked almost pretty. A young man, whom she greeted with an affectionate "Hullo, Bertie" came up to her table and took his seat in a chair facing her. Jocantha looked hard at the new-comer; he was in appearance a few years younger than herself, very much better looking than Gregory, rather better looking, in fact, than any of the young men of her set. She guessed him to be a well-mannered young clerk in some wholesale warehouse, existing and amusing himself as best he might on a tiny salary, and commanding a holiday of about two weeks in the year. He was aware, of course, of his good looks, but with the shy self-consciousness of the Anglo-Saxon, not the blatant complacency of the Latin or Semite. He was obviously on terms of friendly intimacy with the girl he was talking too, probably they were drifting towards a formal engagement. Jocantha pictured the boy's home, in a rather narrow circle, with a tiresome mother who always wanted to know how and where he spent his evenings. He would exchange that humdrum thraldom in due course for a home of his own, dominated by a chronic scarcity of pounds, shillings, and pence, and a dearth of most of the things that made life attractive or comfortable. Jocantha felt extremely sorry for him. She wondered if he had seen the "Yellow Peacock"; the odds were enormously in favour of the supposition that he had not. The girl had finished her tea, and would shortly be going back to her work; when the boy was alone it would be quite easy for Jocantha to say: "My husband has made other arrangements for me this evening; would you care to make use of this ticket, which would otherwise be wasted?" Then she could come there again one afternoon for tea, and, if she saw him, ask him how he liked the play. If he was a nice boy and improved on acquaintance he could be given more theatre tickets and perhaps asked to come one Sunday to tea at Chelsea. Jocantha made up her mind that he would improve on acquaintance, and that Gregory would like him, and that the Fairy Godmother business would prove far more entertaining than she had originally anticipated. The boy was distinctly presentable; he knew how to brush his hair, which was possibly an imitative faculty; he knew what colour of tie suited him, which might be intuition; he was exactly the type that Jocantha admired, which of course was accident. Altogether she was rather pleased when the girl looked at the clock and bade a friendly but hurried farewell to her companion. Bertie nodded "good-bye," gulped down a mouthful of tea, and then produced from his overcoat pocket a paper-covered book, bearing the title "Sepoy and Sahib, a tale of the great Mutiny."

The laws of tea-shop etiquette forbid that you should offer theatre tickets to a stranger without having first caught the stranger's eye. It is even better if you can ask to have a sugar basin passed to you, having previously concealed the fact that you have a large and well-filled sugar basin on your own table; this is not difficult to manage, as the printed menu is generally nearly as large as the table, and can be made to stand on end. Jocantha set to work hopefully; she had a long and rather high-pitched discussion with the waitress concerning alleged defects in an altogether blameless muffin, she made loud and plaintive inquiries about the tube service to some impossibly remote suburb, she talked with brilliant insincerity to the tea-shop kitten, and as a last resort she upset a milk-jug and swore at it daintily. Altogether she attracted a good deal of attention, but never for a moment did she attract the attention of the boy with the beautifully-brushed hair, who was some thousands of miles away in the baking plains of Hindostan, amid deserted bungalows, seething bazaars, and riotous barrack squares, listening to the throbbing of tom-toms and the distant rattle of musketry.

Jocantha went back to her house in Chelsea, which struck her for the first time as looking dull and overfurnished. She had a resentful conviction that Gregory would be uninteresting at dinner, and that the play would be stupid after dinner. On the whole her frame of mind showed a marked divergence from the purring complacency of Attab, who was again curled up in his corner of the divan with a great peace radiating from every curve of his body.

But then he had killed his sparrow

ON APPROVAL

OF all the genuine Bohemians who strayed from time to time into the would-be-Bohemian circle of the Restaurant Nuremberg, Owl Street, Soho, none was more interesting and more elusive than Gebhard Knopfschrank. He had no friends, and though he treated all the restaurant frequenters as acquaintances he never seemed to wish to carry the acquaintanceship beyond the door that led into Owl Street and the outer world. He dealt with them all rather as a market woman might deal with chance passers-by, exhibiting her wares and chattering about the weather and the slackness of business, occasionally about rheumatism, but never showing a desire to penetrate into their daily lives or to dissect their ambitions.

He was understood to belong to a family of peasant farmers, somewhere in Pomerania; some two years ago, according to all that was known of him, he had abandoned the labours and responsibilities of swine tending and goose rearing to try his fortune as an artist in London.

"Why London and not Paris or Munich?" he had been asked by the curious.

Well, there was a ship that left Stolpmünde for London twice a month, that carried few passengers, but carried them cheaply; the railway fares to Munich or Paris were not cheap. Thus it was that he came to select London as the scene of his great adventure.

The question that had long and seriously agitated the frequenters of the Nuremberg was whether this goose-boy migrant was really a soul-driven genius, spreading his wings to the light, or merely an enterprising young man who fancied he could paint and was pardonably anxious to escape from the monotony of rye bread diet and the sandy, swine-bestrewn plains of Pomerania. There was reasonable ground for doubt and caution; the artistic groups that foregathered at the little restaurant contained so many young women with short hair and so many young men with long hair, who supposed themselves to be abnormally gifted in the domain of music, poetry, painting, or stagecraft, with little or nothing to support the supposition, that a self-announced genius of any sort in their midst was inevitably suspect. On the other hand, there was the ever-imminent danger of entertaining, and snubbing, an angel unawares. There had been the lamentable case of Sledonti, the dramatic poet, who had been belittled and cold-shouldered in the Owl Street hall of judgment, and had been afterwards hailed as a master singer by the Grand Duke Constantine Constantinovitch—"the most educated of the Romanoffs," according to Sylvia Strubble, who spoke rather as one who knew every individual member of the Russian imperial family; as a matter of fact, she knew a newspaper correspondent, a young man who ate *bortsch* with the air of having invented it. Sledonti's "Poems of Death and Passion" were now being sold by the thousand in seven European languages, and were about to be translated into Syrian, a circumstance which made the discerning critics of the Nurmberg rather shy of maturing their future judgments oo rapidly and too irrevocably.

As regards Knopfschrank's work, they did not ack opportunity for inspecting and appraising it. However resolutely he might hold himself aloof from the social life of his restaurant acquaintances, he was not minded to hide his artistic performances from their inquiring gaze. Every evening, or nearly every evening, at about seven o'clock, he would make his appearance, sit himself down at his accustomed table, throw a bulky black portfolio on to the chair opposite him, nod round indiscriminately at his fellow-guests, and commence the serious business of eating and drinking. When the coffee stage was reached he would light a cigarette, draw the portfolio over to him, and begin to rummage among its contents. With slow deliberation he would select a few of his more recent studies and sketches, and silently pass them round from table to table, paying especial attention to any new diners who might be present. On the back of each sketch was marked in plain figures the announcement "Price ten shillings."

If his work was not obviously stamped with the hall-mark of genius, at any rate it was remarkable for its choice of an unusual and unvarying theme. His pictures always represented some well-known street or public place in London, fallen into decay and denuded of its human population, in the place of which there roamed a wild fauna, which, from its wealth of exotic species, must have originally escaped from Zoological Gardens and travelling beast shows. "Giraffes drinking at the fountain pools, Trafalgar Square," was one of the most notable and characteristic of his studies, while even more sensational was the gruesome picture of "Vultures attacking dying camel in Upper Berkeley Street." There were also photographs of the large canvas on which he had been engaged for some months, and which he was now endeavouring to sell to some enterprising dealer or adventurous amateur. The subject was "Hyænas asleep in Euston Station," a composition that left nothing to be desired in the way of suggesting unfathomed depths of desolation.

"Of course it may be immensely clever, it may be something epoch-making in the realm of art," said Sylvia Strubble to her own particular circle of listeners, "but, on the other hand, it may be merely mad. One mustn't pay too much attention to the commercial aspect of the case, of course, but still, if some dealer would make a bid for that hyæna picture, or even for some of the sketches, we should know better how to place the man and his work."

"We may all be cursing ourselves one of these days," said Mrs. Nougat-Jones, "for not having bought up his entire portfolio of sketches. At the same time, when there is so much real talent going about, one does not feel like planking down ten shillings for what looks like a bit of whimsical oddity. Now that picture that he showed us last week, 'Sand-grouse roosting on the Albert Memorial,' was very impressive, and of course I could see there was good workmanship in it and breadth of treatment; but it didn't in the least convey the Albert Memorial to me, and Sir James Beanquest tells me that sand-grouse don't roost, they sleep on the ground."

Whatever talent or genius the Pomeranian artist might possess, it certainly failed to receive commercial sanction. The portfolio remained bulky with unsold sketches, and the "Euston Siesta," as the wits of the Nuremberg nicknamed the large canvas, was still in the market. The outward and visible signs of financial embarrassment began to be noticeable; the half-bottle of cheap claret at dinner-time gave way to a small glass of lager, and this in turn was displaced by water. The one-and-sixpenny set dinner receded from an everyday event to a Sunday extravagance; on ordinary days the artist contented himself with a sevenpenny omelette and some bread and cheese, and there were evenings when he did not put in an appearance at all. On the rare occasions when he spoke of his own affairs it was observed that he began to talk more about Pomerania and less about the great world of art.

"It is a busy time there now with us," he said wistfully; "the schwines are driven out into the fields after harvest, and must be looked after. I could be helping to look after if I was there. Here it is difficult to live; art is not appreciate."

"Why don't you go home on a visit?" some one asked tactfully.

"Ah, it cost money! There is the ship passage to Stolpmünde, and there is money that I owe at my lodgings. Even here I owe a few schillings. If I could sell some of my sketches——"

"Perhaps," suggested Mrs. Nougat-Jones, "if you were to offer them for a little less, some of us would be glad to buy a few. Ten shillings is always a consideration, you know, to people who are not over well off. Perhaps if you were to ask six or seven shillings——"

Once a peasant, always a peasant. The mere suggestion of a bargain to be struck brought a twinkle of awakened alertness into the artist's eyes, and hardened the lines of his mouth.

"Nine schilling nine pence each," he snapped, and seemed disappointed that Mrs. Nougat-Jones did not pursue the subject further. He had evidently expected her to offer seven-and-fourpence.

The weeks sped by, and Knopfschrank came more rarely to the restaurant in Owl Street, while his meals on those occasions became more and more meagre. And then came a triumphal day, when he appeared early in the evening in a high state of elation, and ordered an elaborate meal that scarcely stopped short of being a banquet. The ordinary resources of the kitchen were supplemented by an imported dish of smoked goosebreast, a Pomernaian delicacy that was luckily procurable at a firm of *delikatessen* merchants in Coventry Street, while a long-necked bottle of Rhine wine gave a finishing touch of festivity and good cheer to the crowded table.

"He has evidently sold his masterpiece," whispered Sylvia Strubble to Mrs. Nougat-Jones, who had come in late.

"Who has bought it?" she whispered back.

"Don't know; he hasn't said anything yet, but it must be some American. Do you see, he has got a little American flag on the dessert dish, and he has put pennies in the music box three times, once to play the 'Star-spangled Banner,' then a Sousa march, and then the 'Star-spangled Banner' again. It must be an American millionaire, and he's evidently got a big price for it; he's just beaming and chuckling with satisfaction."

"We must ask him who has bought it," said Mrs. Nougat-Jones.

"Hush! no, don't. Let's buy some of his sketches, quick, before we are supposed to know that he's famous; otherwise he'll be doubling the prices. I *am* so glad he's had a success at last. I always believed in him, you know."

For the sum of ten shillings each Miss Strubble acquired the drawings of the camel dying in Upper Berkeley Street and of the giraffes quenching their thirst in Trafalgar Square; at the same price Mrs. Nougat-Jones secured the study of roosting sand-grouse. A more ambitious picture, "Wolves and wapiti fighting on the steps of the Athenæum Club," found a purchaser at fifteen shillings.

"And now what are your plans?" asked a young man who contributed occasional paragraphs to an artistic weekly.

"I go back to Stolpmünde as soon as the ship sails," said the artist, "and I do not return. Never."

"But your work? Your career as painter?"

"Ah, there is nossing in it. One starves. Till to-day I have sold not one of my sketches. To-night you have bought a few, because I am going away from you, but at other times, not one."

"But has not some American——?"

"Ah, the rich American," chuckled the artist. "God be thanked. He dash his car right into our herd of schwines as they were being driven out to the fields. Many of our best schwines he killed, but he paid all damages. He paid perhaps more than they were worth, many times more than they would have fetched in the market after a month of fattening, but he was in a hurry to get on to Dantzig. When one is in a hurry one must pay what one is asked. God be thanked for rich Americans, who are always in a hurry to get somewhere else. My father and mother, they have now so plenty of money; they send me some to pay my debts and come home. I start on Monday for Stolpmünde and I do not come back. Never."

"But your picture, the hyænas?"

"No good. It is too big to carry to Stolpmünde. I burn it."

In time he will be forgotten, but at present Knopfschrank is almost as sore a subject as Sledonti with some of the frequenters of the Nuremberg Restaurant, Owl Street, Soho.